Decae

"I did not dump—" Marjo began.

"And for hitting me over the head with a life jacket and trying to drown me," Matt interrupted.

"I did not—" Chuckling, she tried to pull away from him.

His arm dropped from her shoulders to circle her waist, and he worked his icy fingers inside her shirt to warm them on her goose-pimpled skin. "I will even try to warm you up, Ms. Opaski, not to mention saving you from a sinking boat."

Still smiling, she slipped her own cold fingers inside Matt's shirt. He winced at the chilly touch, but made no objection. "How're you going to warm me up when you're freezing yourself?"

"Give me half an hour," he told her. He glanced at her, then grinned again, with boyish, incorrigible intent. "I have a Plan."

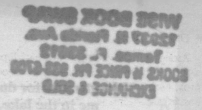
Frances West

Frances West has been writing novels in her head since she was eight years old, when it was called daydreaming and she wondered if it was curable. She's been pleased to discover it's not. She lives in Massachusetts with her husband, son, part-time stepdaughter, a dog, two cats, and six geese.

Other Second Chance at Love books by
Frances West

SOFTER THAN SPRINGTIME #384

Dear Reader:

Along with the beautiful weather, June arrives bearing two wonderfully spirited romances by Second Chance at Love pros, each with her own special flair for wit, humor and — best of all — romance! Author Kelly Adams has yet another hit in her ninth Second Chance at Love romance, *Released Into Dawn* (#440), a captivating tale of sensual friendship and blossoming love. In *Star Light, Star Bright* (#441), Frances West challenges the wounded heart of her heroine with a most irresistable man.

When Annie Maguire finally sees the man she's been waiting a year for — longtime friend Esteban Ramirez — she mistakes him for a reporter and tells him to leave! While they're not exactly off to a good start, both Annie and Esteban are eager to resume the relationship that was interrupted when he was wrongfully imprisoned in South America. But something's changed. Once, he, Annie, and her late husband had been the three musketeers. Now, Esteban's friendly kiss breaks a dam of desire they had both denied for years. Esteban tells Annie he's always loved her; she almost thinks she can see it in his eyes. But is it nostalgia that inspires his passionate response, or could Esteban possibly truly feel as Annie does — hopelessly, beautifully in love. *Released Into Dawn* (#440) is a keeper.

Matt Rutgers is no ordinary hero. A seductive love-song whistler, he's a force to be reckoned with. Adorable and unsuspecting, single mother Marjo Opaski agrees to give Matt and his dog private lessons at her obedience school. Before she knows what's hit her, Marjo's wallet is destroyed, her daughter is upset, and her heart is in serious jeopardy. With Matt, stargazing and romance become the norm in Marjo's previously stable life. But Marjo's daughter resents him. Not only doesn't little Opie want this new guy around *her*, she wants him to stay away from her mother, who's been acting awfully funny since he showed up. Don't worry, though. If anyone can make a happy ending out of all this, it's Frances West. *Star Light, Star Bright* (#441) is a wish come true for a lover of romance.

Berkley has some other stupendous books to offer you this month. In the *New York Times* bestseller *The Spy Wore Red*, the Countess Aline of Romanones relives her incredible adventures as an undercover agent in World War II. Model, spy, Countess — this is the true story of a woman's life in the glittering world of high intrigue. Author Nancy Price has written a powerful, moving thriller in *Sleeping With the Enemy*. Trapped in a cruel, destructive marriage, Sara Burney is desperate to escape her husband's abuse — desperate enough to stage her own death, assume a new identity and "disappear" forever. With all the chilling suspense of Mary Higgins Clark and all the romantic tension of Barbara Michaels, this novel ends in an explosive climax. "Poignant ... an impressive debut," says *Glamour* magazine about *Due East* by Valerie Sayers. Honest, powerful, yet tender, this is the story of Mary Faith Rapple, a smart girl, pretty in a rangy way, who happens to be pregnant. Certainly not unusual, even in the sleepy town of Due East, South Carolina. But when Mary Faith announces that it will be a virgin birth, and her father vows to uncover the truth, the sparks begin to fly! Spirited, evocative — absolutely delightful — *Due East* explores the love, loneliness, hopes, fears and unspoken yearnings of the heart.

A wonderful month for reading. I hope you enjoy this month's Second Chance at Love titles and indulge in these other fine reads. Until next month ...

Happy reading!

Sincerely,

Hillary Cige

Hillary Cige, Editor
SECOND CHANCE AT LOVE
The Berkley Publishing Group
200 Madison Avenue
New York, NY 10016

SECOND CHANCE AT LOVE™

FRANCES WEST
STAR LIGHT, STAR BRIGHT

B

BERKLEY BOOKS, NEW YORK

STAR LIGHT, STAR BRIGHT

First edition published June 1988

ISBN: 0-425-10837-6

"Second Chance at Love" and the butterfly emblem are trademarks belonging to Jove Publications, Inc. The name "BERKLEY" and the "B" logo are trademarks belonging to Berkley Publishing Corporation.

Second Chance at Love books are published by
The Berkley Publishing Group
200 Madison Avenue, New York, NY 10016

Printed in the United States of America

10 9 8 7 6 5 4 3 2 1

To my husband, Bob,
for learning to live on
synonym toast and black copy

STAR LIGHT,
STAR BRIGHT

CHAPTER ONE

OPASKI KENNELS—BOARDING—OBEDIENCE TRAINING.

Matthew Rutgers peered at the sign through the rain-drenched window of his Ford station wagon, then flicked on his directional signal. "This must be it," he announced to the back seat.

An unhappy whimper answered him from behind his shoulder, countered by the slap-slap of windshield wipers and the drumming of rain on the metal roof. The car smelled of wet dog.

"Hey—it's supposed to be the best kennel in Milwaukee," Matt offered. There was no reply but worried silence as he slowed the car to pull into the parking lot. Set back a little from the street was a white clapboard house landscaped with gravel and sturdy, dog-proof bushes. A walkway ran from the side door of the house, marked OFFICE, around to the front. To the left, Matt could see a row of wire-mesh kennel runs, empty now in the pelting rain.

He glanced back at the full-sized, droopy-eared, part bloodhound mutt whose damp fur seemed to be evenly spread over the light blue upholstery. "Come on—you haven't even seen the place yet," Matt commented with a crooked grin. "Trust me. You'll love it."

The dog gave him a baleful look and shifted his weight from one splayed foot to the other.

Matt shook his head, shrugged a pair of broad shoulders, and mumbled, "No sense of humor." He fished into the bag of groceries on the seat beside him and pulled out a nylon leash. A sheet of rain washed down the windshield. Matt peered at it, let out a breath, then stepped out into the weather and jogged around to the back door.

"Come on, boy. Good dog. Come on." He reached in to give a pull on the dog's collar.

Nothing happened.

"Come on, boy. Let's go." The dog's soft whimper escalated into a low, mournful howl.

Cold rain started to seep into the back waistband of Matt's jeans.

He let go of the collar, plunged head and shoulders into the back seat, grabbed two massive front paws, and hauled back. A hundred and eighty pounds of determined man won out over eighty pounds of resisting dog, but as soon as Matt let go of the paws to snap the leash on the hound's collar, the dog scrambled back into a corner of the seat, this time leaving a set of muddy footprints across the fabric.

Matt leaned down, looked his dog in the eye, and stared at him for a long moment. The animal stared back, inching farther into the corner. The worn jeans that had hung loose on Matt's hips when he put them on plastered themselves to his skin, starting at his backside and working down toward his calves.

He let out his breath through his teeth. "All right," he muttered, "we'll do this with brains instead of brawn." With one hand he reached over the seat into the bag of groceries, pulled out the package of steak he'd intended to have for dinner, and ripped off the plastic covering.

Mere seconds later man and dog charged into the front lobby of Opaski Kennels, Matt hauling on the leash and the hound leaping frantically at the package Matt held out in front of him. Behind the counter at one end of the room, two identical blonde heads glanced up sharply as the door swung shut. Matt got a hasty impression of the Bobbsey twins—fluffy blonde curls, two sets of china-blue eyes, matching powder-blue sweat shirts—before the dog leaped up and planted his paws on Matt's chest.

He did a quick two-step to keep his balance and whipped the steak to one side, out of the dog's reach. "Hey! Come on, boy. Down!" The dog dropped to the floor, whimpered, and pranced back and forth, toenails clicking rhythmically on the tiles.

From the counter, two unsmiling faces were watching him. He glanced from one to the other.

Not *quite* identical twins. One was a girl of about ten or eleven, the other more or less grown-up. But they were wearing absolutely identical expressions of incredulous skepticism. He tried a slight grin. The expressions didn't change. The Bobbsey twins, apparently, had no more sense of humor than his dog.

The hound made another leap for the steak. Matt managed to grab his collar and force him down, and the animal sat back and wagged his tail in anticipation, his jaws dropping open. A string of saliva descended lazily to the mud-tracked floor. Two sets of china-blue eyes followed it.

Matt's gaze moved from the dog to the counter to the package of meat that was being studied with single-minded canine determination. He gritted his teeth and grinned.

When he set the package on the floor, the steak disappeared in two gulps.

"Can I help you?" a feminine voice asked blandly.

Matt glanced up. It was the older one who had spoken, and who now regarded him with professional courtesy, pencil poised between two fingers. She looked as if she were carefully resisting any reaction to the scene in front of her. The ten-year-old, on the other hand, was rolling her eyes in an expression Matt recognized: Oh-my-gosh-I-don't-believe-it. His mouth quirked ironically. He didn't quite believe it himself.

The older girl brushed a few strands of blonde hair away from her temple with the pencil eraser. "Are you perhaps looking for the . . . ah . . . obedience school?" she asked, her expression diplomatically blank.

He cleared his throat, muttered, "Yes," then shoved a hand into his pocket and shifted his weight to one foot. Wet jeans pulled taut across his hip. He shook the jeans loose discreetly, with the hand in the pocket, noticing when he glanced down that there were two large pawprints on the front of his jacket. He managed a wry smile. "Is the owner here?"

"I'm Marjo Opaski. I own the kennel, and I also run the obedience-training school."

"Oh?" He frowned at her, surprised. He'd assumed these kids just worked here. She must be older than she looked. He peered at the gaminelike face and dark-lashed blue eyes with suddenly engaged interest. "Oh . . . ah . . . how d'you do. I'm Matt Rutgers. I'd like to see about classes."

"All right. Let me get my book." The blonde head tipped down as she pulled a leather notebook and a stack of index cards from a shelf under the counter. "Dog's name?"

He hesitated. Then, with a half-apologetic shrug, he mumbled, "Flash."

The younger set of blue eyes shot him a look of pained incredulity. It was quelled by a warning glance from her older counterpart.

Marjo Opaski's eyes flicked back to Matt. "Is the

dog full grown?" she asked politely, her pencil poised over a card.

"God, I hope so." The hound now lay on the floor, ears splayed out around his head, contentedly licking the Styrofoam tray that had held the steak. "I've only had him a couple of weeks," Matt explained. "My son got him at a pound in Chicago. He lives there with his mother. Uh—in the city," he added with a grin. "Not at the pound."

"Of course," Marjo Opaski's well-shaped mouth quirked in what looked like it wanted to be a smile, but her voice remained brisk and businesslike.

She didn't *look* old enough, Matt decided, to be so relentlessly serious. He stared at her, assessing her face. She wore no makeup, and with those tousled blonde curls and big blue eyes, in a heart-shaped face, she looked more like a cheerleader than a businesswoman. And there was a quality of vulnerability about her that was decidedly . . . feminine.

The chin lifted and the blue eyes returned the assessment for a brief moment, sending a tiny, surprising but undeniable sizzle of electricity into the air between them. A faint wash of color appeared in Marjo Opaski's cheeks before she dropped her eyes, then leaned forward to look at the dog.

Her sweat shirt pulled momentarily against her body, outlining a pair of generously curved breasts. "Full-sized," she stated.

Matt blinked, then cleared his throat and forcibly suppressed a cough as he realized she was referring to his dog. "Oh—uh, yes. Yes, I'd certainly say so."

Both sets of blue eyes flicked toward him, the expressions doubtful and wary, respectively. "We have classes for adult dogs at seven o'clock on Monday and Thursday evenings," Marjo Opaski told him, "or Wednesday evenings, Saturday afternoons."

There was a sprinkling of freckles across her nose.

She might be in her mid-twenties, he thought. Still pretty young to be running her own business. His gaze wandered down to the front of her sweat shirt again.

She cleared her throat. "Would either of those classes be convenient?" she prompted.

"Oh—convenient—well, no, I'm afraid not. I coach baseball Monday, Wednesday, and Saturday."

The blue eyes regarded him, frowning, then dropped to the notebook. Matt squinted at her, looking for crow's feet. He didn't see any.

"We may have a place open in the puppy classes, held on Sundays . . ."

He shook his head. "I have games on Sunday afternoons."

One eyebrow lifted in polite inquiry. "I assume you're looking for a Tuesday, Thursday, or Friday class, then?"

"Well . . . actually . . ." He smiled and gestured with one hand, palm open. At his feet, Styrofoam crackled as Flash planted a heavy paw firmly on the tray. "I was hoping I could just . . . ah . . . drop him off at a class for dogs, actually."

"Like piano lessons?" The sarcasm was obvious, but the big blue eyes and gamine face took the edge off it. Not to mention the sweat shirt.

"We don't operate that way, Mr. Rutgers," she went on primly. "Training a dog requires a certain *commitment* on the part of the owner, and we insist on it."

"Oh. I see." There was a ripping of Styrofoam, then a crunch as Flash started chewing the tray, scattering small pieces of white foam all over the floor, and trying to swallow the material. "Hey—hey—leave it!" Matt ordered. He crouched down and reached for the tray, but Flash snatched the largest piece of it between his teeth and bounded out of the way, wagging his tail, then leaping back playfully as Matt made another grab for him.

"Flash! Dammit, com'ere!" Matt lunged again, and

the dog skipped sideways and chomped once more on the tray.

"Flash! Drop it!" Matt bellowed.

Marjo Opaski rose from her seat, walked around the end of the counter, stood squarely in the path of the dog, and clapped her hands twice, in front of his nose. Flash dropped the tray and sat back, looking up at her in sheepish apology.

Matt's mouth dropped open in amazement. For Pete's sake, who would have thought that a totally un-armed woman who barely came up to his shoulder could control his dog just by clapping at him with her dainty little hands? She looked as innocent and appealing as Alice in Wonderland, grown up a little. Where had she learned the lion-tamer trick?

She bent over to retrieve the piece of Styrofoam, presenting Matt with a view of a neatly rounded derriere encased in worn blue denim. His expression resolved itself into a silent whistle of approval as he took a step toward her, hand out to his dog.

"The only alternative I see, Mr. Rutgers, is—" She broke off as she spun around and bumped him in the chest with the Styrofoam tray. He steadied her with a hand on her wrist that lingered a few seconds longer than necessary while Marjo Opaski straightened to her full height—about level with his chin, he noticed—and that fascinating trace of color appeared again in her face. "—Private lessons," she finished. There was a small, breathless catch in her voice. She put quick distance between them by moving back around the counter, and Matt's gaze followed her speculatively.

". . . Private lessons," he repeated.

"I could arrange for a five o'clock lesson on Tuesday and Friday, if your schedule would accommodate that."

A lion-tamer with freckles. His mouth curved in a speculative smile. "Yes," he told her. "I think my schedule would . . . accommodate that."

"Tuesday, then." Marjo Opaski gave him a swift, wary glance that was meant, he assumed, to quell his interest. It didn't succeed.

She made a note in her book, then glanced up at him. "You'll need a chain-link training collar large enough to fit easily over the dog's head, and a good, sturdy, six-foot leash."

"All right."

The younger girl was frowning, her gaze shifting back and forth from Marjo Opaski to Matt. He gave her a bland smile and asked, "Are you two sisters?"

"Sisters?" the girl repeated, clearly shocked; then she grinned in amazement, showing even white teeth with a slight gap in the front. "Oh, heck, no!"

Marjo handed Matt a business card with lesson appointments noted, and said evenly, "This is my daughter, Opie." She nodded toward the girl, then glanced back at her notebook.

There was a short silence, during which Matt Rutgers digested the information. "Pleased to meet you, Opie," he said finally, then added, "And you, too, Mrs. Opaski."

"Ms.," she corrected without looking up. "I'm divorced."

"Ahh . . ."

The exclamation was softly spoken, but with enough of a hint of satisfaction to make Marjo Opaski glance up quickly. She caught an unmistakable look of appraisal in Matt Rutgers' eyes, which were warm brown with glints of gold and sparks of humor and something unnameable that elicited a sudden, unbidden response in the region of her stomach. She stared at him, startled, for a long, silent few seconds.

A slow smile of masculine interest spread across his face. "Tuesday, then, Ms. Opaski."

At her slight, mute nod, he grinned again, then turned, grasped his dog by the collar, and dragged him out of the lobby. Canine toenails scraped across the tiled floor.

"Geez..." Opie commented when the door had closed after them. "Some people need a lot of help, huh, Mom?" She shook her hand limply in front of her in a vaudeville gesture that indicated *some people* were hopelessly inept, and pursed her lips in a silent whistle. "I mean, a *lot* of help."

"Mmm."

"Well, you always say it's people like that who keep us in business, huh?"

"Mmm."

"So we'll just begin at the beginning, right? Start with the easy stuff, lesson one, build up his confidence, huh, Mom?"

Marjo's pencil tapped the surface of the desk. She glanced down at the notebook where the Tuesday, 5:00 P.M. slot was filled in with the names *Matt Rutgers* and *Flash*. "I have a feeling," she muttered slowly, "that Mr. Rutgers already has all the—*confidence* he needs."

By 4:55 on Tuesday afternoon, Marjo had decided that overabundant confidence was something she didn't admire. Especially not in a man like Matt Rutgers, with that glint in his eye, and that untrained dog, and that—grin.

She turned on the faucet in the stainless-steel sink that filled one wall of the Opaski Kennels grooming shed and held her hands under the stream of water. Mr. Rutgers, glint in his eye or not, was going to have to concentrate on training his dog. His technique with dogs, heaven knew, could use some concentrated work. He himself was probably as undisciplined and free-wheeling as Flash. The word for Matt Rutgers was... was...

She scowled into the sink, shook her hands, and reached for a towel. She couldn't think of the word, but she knew the type—only too well. Long on good inten-

tions, short on hard work. Likable and good-looking—
and utterly unreliable. Somehow, though, you'd believe
them every time they made a promise and gave you that
easy grin. Or you would if you hadn't learned better.
She might be gullible when it came to men, but she
wasn't a complete fool.

At least not more than once.

She heard the sound of sneakered feet marching
along the gravel walkway outside the workshed. Marjo
looked up from the sink as Opie's blonde head poked in
through the doorway and the voice of ten-year-old authority informed her, "Mo'om. The Beckman's cocker
spaniel has dog food stuck in her ears again."

Marjo gave her daughter a nod and a wry grimace.
"Figures. That dog can't eat a milkbone without getting
crumbs matted in her ears. Would you mind brushing
her out, Ope? I've got a five o'clock lesson."

Opie wrinkled her nose in distaste. "That dog needs a
hairdresser, not a kennel!"

Marjo grinned at her. "You make a great hairdresser,
honey. Don't forget the conditioning mousse and the
platinum blond rinse."

"You forgot to mention the nail polish," Opie muttered, but it was a good-humored complaint.

Marjo smiled at her; then, impulsively, she added,
"Thanks, honey. You're a good kid." Her smile, resting
on her daughter, faded. Opie had to be a good kid—any
child with a father as irresponsible as hers didn't have
much chance of a carefree childhood.

Marjo tossed the damp towel into the laundry bin
beside the sink, turned toward the door, then followed
Opie out into the yard. The two walked side by side
toward the office, Opie's hands stuck in her back
pockets the way Marjo's were, her walk showing the
same purposeful energy. Both of them were dressed in
jeans and sweat shirts, Opie's orange with a logo for a

school soccer team, Marjo's white with a line drawing of Einstein imprinted on the front.

"What's your five o'clock lesson?" the girl asked.

"Matt Rutgers and the mostly bloodhound mutt."

"Oh, *that* one," Opie intoned dramatically.

Marjo flicked her daughter a glance and a sketch of a smile, but said only, "I think I can handle Flash."

"Yeah, sure." Opie grinned back knowingly. "But you've gotta teach the owner how to handle him, Mom . . . that's the catch, huh?"

Marjo shrugged. "Oh—anyone who has an interest in dogs can learn how to handle them." She left it at that. The catch was, of course, that Matt Rutgers' interest seemed to lie . . . elsewhere.

"Whatever you say, Mom. But that Mr. Rutgers—I think he's *hopeless*."

Marjo reached out to ruffle Opie's blonde curls. "Everyone and everything is either *hopeless* or *awesome*. How about a few new adjectives, Ope?"

"Sure, Mom." Opie shrugged nonchalantly. "*Wicked hopeless*."

Marjo rolled her eyes. "Wicked hopeless," she mimicked.

But *hopeless* wasn't the word for Matt Rutgers, either, she reflected as Opie skipped off toward the kennels. He was, if anything, a little too hopeful, with his casual innuendoes. And that *grin*. The word for Matt Rutgers was . . . was . . . poorly trained. Or too sure of himself for his own good. Or his dog's good. Or anyone's good.

She pulled open the door to the office and walked in. Man and dog were waiting for her, the dog standing docilely beside the coffee table, his tail wagging gently across a stack of *Dog's Life* magazines, the man leaning comfortably against her counter, one knee bent, the foot crossed over the other ankle, and the toe of his running shoe propped on the tiled floor. He turned as she came into the room, smiled at her, and slowly straightened up. "Ms. Opaski," he said, his tone not quite serious.

The word was sexy.

The sudden, unbidden thought took her by surprise. Her unguarded glance swept over Matt, head to foot: unruly, slightly-too-long brown hair, broad shoulders, trim, athletic torso beneath a faded tan polo shirt, well-muscled legs in old jeans. A faint, unwanted wash of embarrassment crept into her face as she realized he was watching her look him over, apparently pleased to oblige her. "Mr. Rutgers," she said, her voice a little thin for someone who was not attracted to sexy, irre-sponsible men.

"Call me Matt, if you like."

For some reason, she *didn't* like. She didn't like un-expected thoughts sneaking up on her, she didn't like having him notice that she'd noticed his build, and she didn't want to call him by his first name. But she could hardly refuse without sounding ridiculously stiff. She cleared her throat. "All right. Call me Marjo, then."

"Be glad to." He grinned.

She smiled back, the expression slightly forced, and reminded herself that she was the owner of the best obe-dience school in Milwaukee, and Matt Rutgers was just another dog owner in need of instruction.

She cleared her throat once more and glanced at the dog. Flash's jaw dropped open, and he wagged his tail in pleased greeting, possibly expecting another steak. A copy of *Dog's Life* slid to the floor. Flash sat on it.

"Hey—here, boy—get off that." Matt Rutgers pulled the magazine from under his dog, placed it on the table, and grinned apologetically at Marjo. "Sorry."

She nodded. Just another dog owner. *Badly* in need of instruction.

"The first thing you need to do," she told him, "is to decide what name you're going to call your dog whenever you give an order. Preferably a one-syllable word, for training purposes."

"All right. That's easy. Flash." The dog stood up expectantly, pranced a couple of steps, then lunged for Matt's chest and hit it square in the center. "Hey—" Matt pushed the dog away.

Marjo's eyes lingered, for a moment, on the two pawprints in the middle of the broad chest, while two-syllable words ran through her mind: Body. Shoulders. Biceps. Bedroom.

She glanced up, slammed the mental dictionary shut, then gave Matt Rutgers a coolly professional smile and delivered a slick put-down. "We'll begin, Mr. Rutgers, by deciding who's in charge here. You—or the dog."

"I thought you were going to call me Matt." He smiled engagingly.

"Uh . . . yes . . . *Matt.*" The name stuck in her throat like a wad of cotton. She had a feeling it wasn't just the arrangement of the letters.

She raised her chin a notch and started her standard lecture. "The dog is naturally a pack animal, like the wolf. The inclination to establish a leader/follower role is part of his genetic history. If *you* assume the position of leader, he'll be happy to follow you. If you don't assume it, he'll take it over himself."

Matt nodded seriously, then that slow grin spread across his face. "You want me to assume the role of dominant male . . . uh"—his glance dropped momentarily to the picture of Einstein on the front of her shirt, then flicked back to her eyes—"wolf."

He was flirting with her. In the face of a speech that was supposed to establish a professional tone for an obedience class—a speech that always worked, for heaven's sake—he was flirting with her. There was a smug masculine twist to his mouth, and a cocky lift of one shoulder that told her he was after a response, and that he usually got the one he wanted.

She took a breath and smiled—sweetly. "In point of fact," she informed him, "the dominant wolf in the pack is always female, Mr. Rutgers."

"Female, huh?" He grinned at her, then winked. "Call me Matt."

Good grief. The man was unsquashable. He must have an ego like a brand-new marshmallow. "Uh... yes. *Matt*. What you want to convey to the dog...uh ... *Matt* ... is that you are the leader."

He nodded agreeably. "Do I tell him about his genetic history, or do I just growl at him?"

She gave him a tight smile. "Why don't you start with the command to heel. You have the training collar?"

Matt glanced at the dog, then gave Marjo a sidelong look as he fished into the back pocket of his jeans and pulled out the chain-link collar. "This is it, Flash, boy. Heavy artillery."

The dog cocked his head, sniffed anxiously, then whimpered.

Marjo stared levelly at his owner. "Mr. Ru—" She closed her eyes, then opened them again and smiled. "*Matt*. A training collar is essential. Used properly, it won't hurt the dog. If you give it to me, I'll demonstrate." Flash wagged his tail nervously as his master handed over the collar. "There are two rings here, you notice," she explained. "You slide the chain through the larger ring to make a loop."

Matt examined it dubiously. "Like . . . a noose."

"Uh . . . yes."

He glanced from the collar to the dog, then back to Marjo. "Look, he may have a few bad habits"—he gestured with one hand—"well, all right, he may have a lot of bad habits, but . . . hanging?" The brown eyes regarded her with skepticism and a hint of uncalled-for amusement. Marjo decided it was beneath her notice.

"The idea," she told him coolly, "is to provide an

element of surprise that will make him stop and take notice of what he's expected to do. A sharp tug on the collar—not steady pressure. Believe me, if you use it properly, the effect won't be any more than surprising, but that element is essential if you intend to control the dog."

Matt raised an eyebrow at her, then gave the dog an ironic nod. "Heavy artillery."

"Mr. Rutgers," Marjo said, her teeth clenched against rising irritation, "we do not use 'heavy artillery' here. Obedience training is based on cooperation and trust. *And* on the proper attitude. We take teaching seriously, here, and no matter what you do for a living—"

"I'm a teacher," he interrupted her. "High school physics."

A teacher. Good grief. She had a mental image of a classroom full of students all behaving like Flash, while Matt Rutgers lured them down from windowsills and desktops with hamburgers and french fries. "Oh. Well. I . . . you—" She broke off, took another breath and started again. *"Matt.* I don't know how you teach your students, but here—"

"You'll be relieved to learn that I haven't yet found it necessary to hang any of them," he told her. The teasing glint was back in his eye, infuriating, outrageous, and far too appealing to be acknowledged. She stared at him, utterly at a loss for words, while he grinned insouciantly. "On the other hand, I haven't taught any of them to heel, either."

The man was impossible. He was flip and irreverent and infuriating, and the worst of it was that she realized, dimly, that her own reaction to him had something to do with that very male torso and that very confident . . . grin.

She blinked, dragged her disappearing composure back by its coattails, and reminded herself that this was an obedience lesson.

"Let's get started, okay?" she said shortly.

Matt Rutgers shrugged his broad shoulders and grinned at her. "Sure."

With instruction, he managed to get the collar on the dog, attach the leash, and get out the door, Flash more or less at heel, but when the hound caught scent of the kennels to his right, he charged toward them like a canine bulldozer, all his instincts geared to towing behind him whatever was there. It happened to be Matt.

Instead of applying the sharp tug she'd taught him, Marjo watched Matt haul back on the leash with steady but ineffective pressure as Flash strained toward the kennels, collar tight around his neck, tongue hanging out as his breathing became labored and audible.

"Wait a minute! Stop! Stop!"

Matt dragged the dog to a halt and looked back at her.

"One sharp tug!" Marjo reiterated. "Then let up the pressure. You want to surprise him, not choke him. Now come back this way. A single, hard tug. Got it?"

"Right," he muttered. But the next try was a repeat of the first. Marjo let out an exasperated breath as canine and man fought at cross purposes, both superbly muscled physiques straining in opposite directions.

"Stop!" she ordered again. She marched toward them, each footstep crunching with determination on the gravel. "All you're accomplishing here is choking him."

"*I'm* choking him? He's pulling at least as hard as I am. I'd describe it as a team effort."

"Well, whatever it is, it's *not* teaching him to heel."

He stared back at her, then gave a shrug—easygoing, confident, male. "Look—the training collar was *your* idea, not mine."

"Of course it was," she told him, too distinctly. "It's obvious that no idea remotely connected to training a dog has ever entered your head."

"It's not exactly a topic that occupies my every waking thought, no."

"Well, it occupies quite a few of *my* waking thoughts, Mr. Rutgers, and I take it seriously!"

"I'll say," he muttered. "You'd think a smile would crack your face."

"I can smile perfectly well when it's appropriate."

"When it's *appropriate?*" His eyebrows rose in disbelief, then an amazed grin split his features, and he gave a deep belly laugh of genuine amusement, rocking back on his heels in enjoyment. "You make it sound like French kissing."

Marjo flushed scarlet. "Mr. Rutgers," she stated with as much dignity as she could manage in the face of that uninhibited laughter, "I don't think we can work together. I'll refer you to another kennel." She reached into her pocket, pulled out a worn leather wallet, and fumbled through it, her fingers shaking with outrage. She pulled out a business card and dropped the wallet. Flash made a dive for it.

"Give me that!" Marjo muttered inelegantly, snatching her wallet from the dog's jaws.

"Look," Matt started, his laughter dying down to a chuckle. "Can't we—"

"Here." She thrust the card at him. "Maybe the instructors at this school will have—uncrackable faces." She stuffed the stack of cards into her wallet in one lump. The wallet wouldn't close, but she shoved it into her pocket anyway and spun on her heel to make an exit. Two steps later, the wallet hit the ground, scattering its contents over the gravel.

"Oh, *dammit!*" she swore under her breath as she turned back. But Matt Rutgers was already bending to retrieve the wallet, and she had to wait for him to straighten up, business cards and wallet in his hands.

"Ms. Opaski, I apologize," he told her, the smile carefully wiped from his face—though not, she noticed, from his eyes. He crammed everything back into her wallet, making a messy job of it because he was watching her and not his hands. "Please don't kick me out of your obedience school. I'll behave. I'll make a serious effort. I won't choke my dog. Give us another chance."

The plea was so absurdly earnest that, in spite of herself, Marjo offered no resistance when he reached for her hand, pulled it out in front of her, palm upward, and pressed her bulging wallet into it. "We're desperate, Ms. Opaski."

Both his hands were clasped around hers, the grip warm and strong and masculine, and not in the least apologetic. There was a funny tightening of the muscles in her throat and a sudden drop in the pit of her stomach that she recognized clearly. Her gaze moved from their clasped hands along his forearm, up to his shoulder, then to his face.

He let go of her, folded his hands chastely behind his back, and regarded her solemnly, only the brown eyes betraying a glint of humor that was, after all, and in spite of her bruised dignity, irresistible.

By slow degrees, the corners of her mouth turned up. She shook her head, then gave a reluctant huff of laughter. "You're right. You *are* desperate."

"We are. You can't turn away a desperate man, can you? Or a desperate dog?"

She looked at him, shook her head again, and took a breath. "Oh, well. I guess I wouldn't be much of a trainer if I turned away a desperate dog."

His lips curved in a self-satisfied grin that lingered on her face just long enough to let her know he liked what he saw despite the fact that it was unadorned with makeup or jewelry.

More than long enough to let her know her hormones were still in working order.

Marjo turned her gaze hastily to the desperate dog

and held out her hand for the leash. "Why don't I demonstrate what I mean by a sharp tug?" she offered.

Matt took her wallet while she got the dog into position at her left side. "Flash, heel!" she ordered, then set off briskly toward the corner of the building. The bloodhound followed her a few steps, then dashed in front of her. Marjo dropped the slack in the leash, let Flash get up six feet of momentum, then yanked back on the leash as he reached the end of it. He gave a short, surprised yelp as he was brought to an abrupt stop, then turned and looked at her in puzzled discontent.

Marjo did an about-face, said, "Heel!", and walked briskly back toward Matt. Flash followed for a few paces at the pull of the leash, then, as before, forged ahead. She repeated the sharp stop and the about-face, and when she ordered, "Heel!" for the third time, the dog walked meekly beside her across the yard.

Matt was watching in unfeigned amazement. "Unbelievable," he commented.

She handed him the leash. "Give it a try."

Fifteen minutes later, Matt had the dog heeling reasonably well, and Marjo, satisfied, led the way back to the office. Matt Rutgers made no more off-the-cuff remarks for the rest of the lesson, but when Marjo dropped her wallet on a chair in the lobby and walked to the counter to get her receipt book, he followed her, the look in his eyes speculative enough to send a disturbing prickle along her spine. He leaned over the counter to watch her fill out his receipt.

"I have to say, Ms. Opaski, that you know what you're doing around dogs."

Her pulse quickened a beat. She glanced at him briefly, then looked down again. "Thanks."

"Must be something to this female dominance theory," he observed.

"I beg your pardon?"

He leaned closer, grinning at her from a distance of six inches. "You know, with the wolves."

The teasing twinkle was back in his eye, the grin beguiling and devilish, and her pulse quickened another beat. "I . . . don't think that's it. I know quite a few men who are very good with dogs."

"Do you, now?" He grinned. "And how many do you know who aren't?"

Good grief. He made it sound as if she had some kind of male harem. Silence seemed the only safe answer. She tore off the receipt and handed it to him.

Flash, realizing that he was being ignored, sniffed at the stack of *Dog's Life* magazines, then crossed the room to nose into the chairs on the other side.

Matt folded the slip of paper and put it in his pocket, then leaned over the counter again. "Would you have dinner with me, Ms. Opaski?"

A surge of purely feminine elation brought warmth to her face. She checked it swiftly, appalled that her first reaction was to say yes. "I'm sorry. I'm having dinner with my daughter."

"Bring her along."

"I . . ." She searched for an excuse, her mind blank for a moment before she realized the simple truth would do. "Opie doesn't take easily to . . . people she doesn't know."

Matt was silent for a moment, his gaze resting on her thoughtfully. Then he straightened, smiled easily, and said, "Some other time, then."

She didn't answer him directly. "I'll see you Friday. Five o'clock."

"We'll be here."

Marjo watched him walk out, the dog trailing behind him in nothing resembling a heel position, but walking, at least, under his own power. Progress of a sort, she thought dryly. He wasn't, at any rate, *hopeless*.

The pencil in her fingers tapped the counter top.

What *would* Opie make of Matt Rutgers, if she got to know him? Marjo sighed once. The truth was that Opie wasn't just slow to warm up, she was slow—very slow —to give her trust. She'd had it betrayed too often.

The pencil tapped again on the counter. Marjo drew in a deep breath, then let the pencil drop from her fingers. Opie wasn't the only one who'd been betrayed by empty promises and forgotten obligations. In the end, all the charm and good looks in the world had counted for little when measured beside the security of a place she could call her own and a paycheck she could count on because she'd earned it herself.

She'd made a point, in the three years since her divorce, of being interested in dependability, maturity, and regular habits. Matt Rutgers didn't fit her requirements.

Her mouth firmed into a decided line, Marjo picked up her pencil, got out her accounts-receivable book, and dismissed Matt Rutgers from her mind.

Five minutes later, she realized the wallet was missing from the chair where she'd left it.

CHAPTER TWO

FIVE MINUTES AFTER he left Opaski Kennels, Matt Rutgers pulled onto Lake Drive, the tree-lined parkway that skirted the shore of Lake Michigan past the downtown area of Milwaukee, then connected with the cross-city freeway to West Allis, the comfortably affluent section of the city where Matt owned a rambling stone house and half an acre of what had been, before he'd acquired a dog, a moderately well-kept yard.

He glanced back at Flash, who was lying docilely across the back seat, only occasional chewing sounds testifying to his presence.

"Well, that wasn't so bad—huh, Flash, boy?"

The dog chewed again. Something hit the floor with a soft thud.

Matt shot a quick glance over his shoulder. "What have you got there?" It was something brown. Leathery. Chewed bits of it littered the seat.

He risked a traffic accident to look again.

"Oh, no." He turned back to the road. "No," he muttered at the windshield in front of him. "No, this can't be true." He ran a hand through his hair, then shook his head, still muttering. "No animal could be this much trouble." He flicked on his directional and slowed to pull off the road. "Not even this one." The driver behind him gave Matt a look of exaggerated pity and a slow shake of his head as he passed.

The wallet was in shreds, the contents shredded to match. Business cards bearing the names of kennels, veterinary clinics, and dog grooming services were scattered soggily across the floor; a Visa card dented with tooth marks lay under one of Flash's paws.

Matt glanced up from his survey of the damage and glared at the dog. The mutt grinned happily at him, drooling on the car seat.

Matt rubbed the bridge of his nose between thumb and forefinger and turned back to the windshield. The damned animal seemed to *know* he was untouchable. A dog given to a father by his only son could simply not be taken back to the pound. "So when I'm not around, you won't be lonely," Tim had said. What was a father supposed to do?

He let out a long sigh. What he had done was swallow the lump in his throat and crouch down to put one arm around Timmy's shoulders and the other around the dog.

The truth was that he *had* been lonely. Even before the divorce, he'd been lonely—from the time that Timmy had started first grade and Anne had taken a job in Chicago, where there was more scope for her expanding law practice. She'd found it necessary to stay in the city for an occasional night. Then the nights had been not-so-occasional, and she'd taken an apartment for convenience. Their divorce, he'd realized with slow and painful clarity, was only a formalization of what had already happened, and when he'd finally admitted that the marriage was over, he'd had to acknowledge that it was inevitable. Ambition like Anne's could never be compatible with his own choice for life in the slow lane.

Matt glanced back one more time at the shredded

wallet, then passed a hand over his eyes and sighed again. The slow lane had speeded up a little since he'd acquired this dog. And he was beginning to suspect that loneliness was nothing compared to life with Timmy's dog.

He pulled out into the traffic again, wondering where he could find a department store that sold wallets.

Two hours later, he parked his station wagon in the empty lot of Opaski Kennels. The office was closed, but there was a light in one of the upstairs windows, where a white ruffled curtain hung partly open. Matt stared up at it, wondering if Marjo Opaski had a sense of humor to match her freckles and her lion-tamer act. His mouth quirked in a wry grin. She *had* agreed he was desperate.

He reached for the department store bag, then got out of the car and walked around the corner of the building to the front entrance of the house. Flash had been left at home, tied, he hoped, securely.

The name OPASKI in garish yellow and purple letters was hand printed on a wooden sign, over a coat of arms featuring a German shepherd flanked by miniature poodles. Matt smiled slightly, recognizing a ten-year-old's taste when he saw it, and rang the bell.

He heard footsteps on an inside staircase, then the door swung back, and Opie stood in the hallway looking up at him.

"Oh," the girl greeted him, with straightforward disregard of convention. "You must be here with the wallet."

Matt glanced down at the bag in his hand. "Not exactly, but you're close." Opie peered at the bag curiously. When she made no move away from the doorway, he asked, "Can I come in?"

She shrugged and stepped aside, then called up the stairs, "It's Mr. Rutgers, Mom."

"Okay," Marjo called from the second floor as Matt

followed Opie up to the landing. The girl led the way into a small living room comfortably furnished in muted shades of beige, brightened with artwork and crafts, in which Matt recognized Opie's hand. A wall hanging of woven grass and yarn filled the space above the couch, the predominant colors yellow and purple.

Marjo appeared in a doorway that evidently led to the kitchen, wiping her hands on a dish towel. "Hello," she offered. Politely, Matt decided, but with little evidence that she was glad to see him.

"Hi." His gaze lingered speculatively on her face, as he assessed her mood. One corner of his mouth turned up crookedly. "I'm here about the wallet."

Her face took on a *don't-tell-me* expression. *"About the wallet?"*

"Yes. As in, 'about the remains of what was formerly your wallet.'"

Opie coughed theatrically, pounding on her chest with one fist.

"Oh," Marjo commented. Politely.

He held out the bag. "I replaced the wallet, but I'm afraid I couldn't do much about the credit cards or your license. What's left of them is in there."

"Well." She took the bag, then glanced into it, made a slight grimace, and set it on the bookshelf next to her. Her restraint told him all he needed to hear. More than he needed to hear, actually.

"I'm . . . ah . . . afraid he did a pretty good job."

She gave him a watered-down version of her professional smile. "I suppose that's one of the hazards of the business. I shouldn't have left it on a chair where he could reach it." She added with relentless courtesy, "Thank you for the new wallet."

Opie poked through the bag and came up with the tooth-marked Visa card. "Geez . . . " She turned the card over in her fingers, held it up to the light to verify that the holes did, indeed, go all the way through, and shook her head. "Ho, boy. I mean, ho *boy*."

Marjo gave her a look of parental tolerance. Matt smiled uncomfortably, shoved his hands into his pockets, and wondered if he should make a stab at restoring whatever image he had with Marjo. He shot a quick, appraising glance at her face, then his gaze drifted down over the bust of Einstein and snug, pleasingly filled-out jeans. He cleared his throat. "Nice apartment," he commented.

"Thank you."

He scanned the bookshelves that lined one wall beneath Opie's artwork. "You must like books."

"Yes. We like books."

His gaze lingered on her again. "What kind of books?"

"Oh"—she made a gesture with the dish towel—"a lot of dog books, a little of everything else."

"Maybe I should have read some of the dog books. I *am* sorry—about the wallet."

Opie gave Matt a sidelong look and shook her head over the credit card.

"It's all right—really."

The wall of courtesy between them didn't seem to have a chink. Matt examined Marjo with a solemnity that matched her own *Miss Manners* deportment, then added, "I've told Flash the cost of the new one will come out of his allowance."

Marjo's mouth finally curved in a smile. "Honestly, you are desperate, aren't you?"

"Believe me, since I got that dog, I've discovered levels of desperation I never suspected," he said with fervor.

Unexpected laughter bubbled up in her throat. She leaned forward from the waist, shoulders shaking, the dish towel dangling from her fingers, then looked up at him with a grin that was reflected, engagingly, in the blue eyes. "Take heart," she told him. "After he learns to heel, we'll work on not chewing up small leather objects."

"Ms. Opaski," he told her, grinning back, "I would be very grateful if you would work with us on not chewing up small leather objects."

She chuckled, then stood looking back at him, warmed by the glint of humor in the brown eyes. The man *was* unsquashable. Not to mention persistent. And that *was* flattering. And he *was* likable. And Opie *had* done her best to insult him.

Marjo shrugged slightly, gave a half-smile, then gestured toward the kitchen with the dish towel and gave in to a quick, uncharacteristic impulse. "Would you like a cup of coffee?"

"I'd love a cup of coffee," he told her.

Opie included them both in a look of disbelief, then announced, "I'm going to watch TV," and dropped the credit card ostentatiously on the bookshelf.

Marjo watched her daughter's expressive exit with equal parts exasperation and amusement, then shook her head and led the way into the kitchen.

Matt leaned against the counter while she filled the tea kettle with water, turned on the burner, and got out cups and instant coffee. His gaze roved around the room, stopping on the table, where a single candle in a wooden holder was still burning.

"I didn't interrupt your dinner, did I?"

"Oh, no, I was just clearing the dishes."

"You and Opie always eat by candlelight?"

She shrugged reticently. "Yes, most of the time. We like it."

"That's nice," he said. His smile was friendly, his interest open as he took in the cheerful yellow walls displaying more of Opie's artwork, the plain wooden table, Marjo's colorful stoneware dishes. "I take it Opie's the artist in the house?"

"That's right. I squander all my own creativity on training dogs."

"And nothing else?"

"Nope. Unless you count Parcheesi tournaments." She grinned. "Which I usually lose."

"To Opie." He acknowledged her nod with a slight smile, then his glance flicked around the walls once more. "Is Opie a nickname from Opaski?"

Marjo's gaze dropped a little too abruptly to the stove. "No. Opaski is my maiden name. Opie is short for Ophelia." She shoved her hands into her pockets, the gesture revealingly stiff, before she added, "Wozniak. Ophelia Wozniak."

There was a measurable silence while Marjo stared at the stove. Self-consciously, she pulled her hands out of her pockets.

The kettle whistled, and she filled the cups. "Cream and sugar?"

"Just sugar." She offered him the sugar bowl and a spoon, and he murmured, "Thanks."

She watched him stir sugar into his coffee, the simple domestic act pricking her memory. Stan had taken his with two sugars, no cream. *She'd* been expected to add the sugar. *And* pick up the cup and wipe the table, just as her mother had always done for her father. When she'd married Stan, she'd taken on the domestic role without a second thought. The second thoughts had come later.

Matt glanced up to catch her expression as she watched him, and she gestured, feeling awkward, toward one of the kitchen chairs. "Sit down."

He nodded and carried his cup to the table. She took the chair opposite him, folding one knee up in front of her, hooking a heel on the edge of her chair.

His curly, dark hair gleamed with candlelight, his eyes reflected tiny gold glints as he studied her over the rim of his cup. A shiver of feminine awareness ran down her spine. He *was* good-looking. As good-looking as Stan was, and with the same air of cocky masculine assurance that had been so impossible to resist when she'd been seventeen. She swallowed down the feeling with a mouthful of coffee, surprised and disturbed by the purely physical attraction that fluttered in her stomach. She thought she'd outgrown that reaction when she'd outgrown her marriage.

"So," he said easily. "You own your own kennel, Ms. Opaski."

Her shoulders lifted in a diffident shrug. "Me and the bank. This was a run-down duplex when I bought it. I convinced the bank to give me a business loan to renovate the downstairs." She smiled slightly. "A *modest* business loan. But as the kennel got going, my credit improved, fortunately."

"It's not easy to start a small business and make it profitable."

"We worked hard."

One eyebrow rose inquisitively. "You and Opie?"

"Yes. Me and Opie."

He nodded, as if the fact of her partnership with Opie was unquestioned. "Nice that you can make your own living this way."

"Yes," she said again; then, with another brief smile, admitted, "I love the work. And in just twenty-two years the mortgage will be paid off."

"Twenty-two years, huh?" He leaned back, his eyes narrowed at her. "Let's see, that means you'll be about . . . forty-eight?"

"Fifty. If anyone's counting."

"What makes you think anyone's counting?" he asked with feigned innocence.

She studied him a moment, glanced down at the table, then looked up again. "When you're twenty-eight and have a ten-year-old daughter, you get the feeling sometimes that people are counting."

He set down his coffee cup. "I wasn't thinking of Opie."

He seemed to mean it. His gaze was nonjudgmental —interested but not avid—waiting, it seemed, for her to tell her own story.

She glanced away from him, not quite easy with sharing such private details of her life. "What will *you* be doing in twenty-two years?"

"Hmm." He considered. "I'll still be teaching high school physics, I hope. But I'll own a new eighteen-foot outboard, rigged out for fishing. And if there's any justice in the world, my ball team will be winning a pennant."

"I take it they're not winning now?"

"Eleventh place. Out of twelve."

"Oh." She gave a chuckle of sympathy. "Well, there's always next year."

"Or some year, anyway, if there's any justice in the world." He grinned. "And by that time, if there's any justice in the world, Flash will be spending his sunset years lying on the porch and not chewing up wallets."

"Flash," she informed him, "will be perfectly trained in six months."

He raised an eyebrow in hopeful but disbelieving inquiry. "And my life will be peaceful?"

"I don't know. Was it peaceful before you got a dog?"

"Well, relatively." He sipped his coffee. "Was yours peaceful before you owned a kennel, Ms. Opaski?"

She lowered her coffee cup to the table and stared into it, the smile disappearing swiftly from her face. "No."

He waited for her to go on, watching as she twisted the cup around in slow circles on the table. "No?" he asked finally.

"No." She pushed back the chair with sudden energy

and stood up. "Would you like a piece of cake? Opie made it this afternoon."

"Sure," he said agreeably, quelling his curiosity.

The cake was a four layer, somewhat free-form creation frosted with chocolate fudge icing and decorated with pink and green flowers. "Lemon-chocolate-raisin-spice cake," she said as she set it on the table.

Matt regarded it with awe.

"Opie tends toward the dramatic," Marjo explained.

He glanced up at her, carefully suppressing a smile. "I love drama."

He claimed to love the cake, too. "Best lemon-chocolate-raisin-spice cake I ever had," he told her with his mouth full.

"Had a lot of lemon-chocolate-raisin-spice cake, have you?"

"I've had my share of exotic food," he admitted. "My son was a Doctor Seuss fan. For a while, all he'd eat for breakfast was green eggs and ham."

"Green eggs and ham?" She had to laugh. "Oh, no. Not first thing in the morning."

"Bright and early. Scrambled eggs with green food coloring. Timmy's mother would hide behind the newspaper so she wouldn't have to watch us eat."

Marjo flicked him a bemused glance, trying to picture the family breakfast tableau in reverse: Mom reading the paper, Dad dishing up the eggs. It wasn't a scene that came readily to mind. She herself couldn't even remember sitting down at a family breakfast when Opie had been at the Doctor Seuss stage. She'd been too busy hovering, supplying more coffee and making sure Opie didn't spill her juice or spit out her cereal. If she had, it would always, somehow, have been Marjo's fault.

"How old is Timmy?" she asked.

"He's ten."

"Ten?" she repeated, jolted. "Opie's age?"

"Yes."

She hadn't pictured him with a ten-year-old. "He lives in Chicago?"

"Mmm. During the week. He's with me weekends and school vacations," he said matter-of-factly. "And summers."

"All summer, too?" she let slip, her disbelief obvious.

Matt looked up at her, puzzled. "Yes."

Marjo's glance flickered away from him in embarrassment. She shouldn't have asked. But the idea of Matt Rutgers as an active father was unsettling. It didn't fit her preconceptions of the man.

She got up from the table under the pretext of carrying the cake to the counter and setting the cake lid back on the plate. The truth was that the idea of any man as an active father was alien to her. Her own father's idea of parental responsibility had stopped at bringing home his weekly paycheck, which was all she'd ever expected from Stan.

And Stan had never even managed that much.

"Opie spends her summers here?" Matt asked casually into the awkward silence.

"Opie spends all her time here." She flicked a crumb off the counter, then reached for the sponge to wipe the already clean surface, her spine stiffened against Matt Rutger's gaze, angry at herself for reacting to the simple question. Dammit, why should she feel guilty and apologetic because Opie's father couldn't manage the responsibility of holding down a steady job? Yet she did, just as she had felt guilty all the years of her failing marriage. For not being the perfect, uncomplaining wife. For not being able to keep the marriage together. For having gotten pregnant in the first place. It had never, as far as she knew, occurred to Stan Wozniak that the event required two participants.

She gave the counter a vicious swipe and tossed the sponge into the sink, then forced herself to turn around.

Her smile was brittle. "Thanks for the new wallet," she told Matt coolly, the words clearly dismissive, her voice hard and defiant.

Matt studied her in silence for a long moment. "She seems like a nice kid," he said finally. "I'd say you've done a good job with her."

The sudden lump in her throat took Marjo by surprise. She blinked, forcing back a wave of emotion that left her control shaky and her façade of indifference crumbling. She had to turn back to the sink, making a production of hanging the dish towel on a hook and straightening plates on the shelves. Somehow Matt Rutgers—with his good humor and his tolerance of ten-year-olds and his green eggs—had gotten under her guard, brought up emotions she didn't want to deal with, and threatened the tight, closed mother-daughter circle that had formed her security—and Opie's—for three years. And it was no one's fault but her own. She'd invited him in here . . . fed him Opie's cake . . .

"Listen," she said, her voice gruff, "I've got to check on the dogs before it gets too dark, so . . ." She glanced at him over her shoulder to find him looking back at her, his hand resting at the side of his plate, the cake not quite finished.

He forked up the last bite of it, then stood and brought his plate to the counter, where he set it down beside the sink. "Look, I'm sorry."

She gave a false laugh and waved a hand in the air. "Oh, about the wallet, you really—"

"No. About bringing up a subject you don't want to talk about."

She swallowed again, not trusting her voice. Her gaze moved from the plate, which he'd brought—himself—to the sink, up along his beautifully muscled torso to the all-American face and the brown eyes that stared back at hers with honest apology. He was too good to be believed. Entirely too perfect to be trusted, though for the life of her she could find no flaw other than his owning a dog who chewed up wallets. She looked down again, staring into the sink. "You didn't exactly bring up the subject," she conceded. "I mean, it's perfectly natural to wonder what—you know—"

"You don't owe me any explanations, Marjo."

"I—well—then I guess you don't owe me any apologies, either."

He grinned. "Deal. So how 'bout you show me around the kennels while you check on the dogs?"

She hesitated a moment, then let out a breath, pushing her hands into the back pockets of her jeans. It was a simple enough request—easy, friendly, open. Like the man himself. Hard to fault, despite her overactive defenses. And hard not to like, with that crooked grin, and the ready humor in his eyes, and his untroubled acceptance of the fact that her life history didn't exactly represent every young girl's dream. She glanced at him again. "Well . . . if you're really interested."

"I'm interested."

The sky was streaked with rose at the western horizon as Marjo and Matt walked around the side of the building toward the kennels. Their footsteps crunched on the gravel in unison, making a sharp counterpoint to the muted sounds of the spring evening. A soft breeze carried the faintly disinfectant smell of the kennels and the twittering of evening birds.

From a lilac bush beside the house, a wren scolded them. Matt turned his head toward it as they walked by, grinning at the aggressive little bird, but he made no comment. Marjo glanced at him, then shoved her hands into her pockets, not quite at ease with the sense of intimacy invoked by the quiet evening.

As they approached a new, one-story addition to the house, she gestured toward it. "That's the grooming shed. We added it on last year so we could enlarge the inside training room. Now we can have classes all year."

"In case any of your clients have dogs that misbehave in the winter?"

"Mmm." She smiled briefly. "There's really more demand for classes in winter than any other season."

"All those desperate dog owners cooped up with the beasts for months."

"Something like that." She opened the door to the grooming shed, flicked the switch for the fluorescent lights, and stood aside for Matt to look in. A stainless-steel sink and grooming table reflected light from spotlessly clean surfaces; shelves of brushes, bottles, and neatly folded towels ranged along one wall. Two oversized hair dryers were mounted over the table.

Matt made a sound of approval. "You're pretty well equipped here, looks like."

"Thanks." She glanced around the impeccably kept room with obvious pride. "It makes grooming a whole lot easier." She switched off the light. "The kennels are this way." A door at the back corner of the building led to a long, narrow corridor of dog kennels, each with an outside run. Investigative canine scuffling greeted them as they walked in. At the end of the kennels, an excitable cocker spaniel yipped and jumped at them, ears flapping.

"The one making all the noise is Dicey. Opie calls her Princess Di, because she requires so much attention."

Matt chuckled appreciatively, then followed her toward Dicey's kennel. Marjo crouched down to scratch the cocker's ears and croon soothing nonsense to the little dog. Dicey sighed in contentment.

Marjo moved down the line of kennels, speaking to each dog while Matt ambled along beside her.

"Was this your life ambition? To own a kennel?" he asked.

"No, I wanted to be a vet." She smiled. "Either that or a cheerleader for the Green Bay Packers. But I'm happy with Dicey and the crew."

"That's an achievement in itself—to love what you do for a living. Especially when you've done it all on your own."

"Oh, well." She gave a self-conscious shrug. "I didn't have much choice about that part."

"No," he agreed. "Sometimes you don't."

She glanced at him sharply, wondering if he expected her to fill in the rest of the story, but he was stretching his hand out to a friendly German shepherd, bending down to mutter, "Good boy."

"She's a she," Marjo pointed out.

"Good girl," he amended without missing a beat.

One corner of Marjo's mouth curled up in a half-smile. There was something about Matt Rutgers' cheerful acceptance of his own failings that was... endearing. The more so because it took her by surprise every time. She couldn't remember Stan ever once admitting he had a fault. Nor her father, either, for that matter. She'd grown up believing that the male ego needed coddling.

Matt stood up straight, running a hand through his hair, and glanced back along the orderly row of kennels, then smiled in approval at Marjo. "First-class accommodations, I'd say. I've been threatening Flash with a boarding kennel, but if this is any example of one, maybe I should have been holding it out as a reward."

"Do you have a kennel for him at home?" She met his eyes with another smile as she led the way out into the darkening spring evening.

"Not yet. I've only had him two-and-a-half weeks."

"You didn't know you were getting him?"

"Uh-uh. He was a surprise from Timmy. Anne—my ex-wife—tried to talk him out of it, but he was so excited about the idea that she didn't have the heart to tell him no."

His tone of voice was philosophical and indulgent—with no hint of the resentment she would have expected. She slanted a look at him, but his face was shadowed, back-lit by the western sky, where streaks of pink and rose were fading into the darkening violet overhead, and the first stars were offering faint glimmers.

"What does she do?" Marjo asked before she could stop herself.

"She's a lawyer. On her way up. She moved to Chicago because it gave her more scope for her law practice." The words, again, were spoken with no discernible bitterness. He glanced at her, his face unreadable in the dim light, then ambled to a stop, turning to look toward the sunset, standing silent for a moment. "Look at that sky," he murmured.

She gazed toward it, seeing not the sky but the outline of his shoulder, the edge of his jaw, the disheveled, curly hair at his temple.

"Nice, huh?" he commented.

"Yes . . . nice."

He gave her a glance and a brief, companionable smile, then resumed walking along the gravel toward the front door of the house. He paused at the doorway and turned toward her, thumbs hooked into the waistband of his jeans. "Thanks for the tour."

"You're welcome," she said truthfully. "I like showing the place off." She pushed her own hands into her back pockets, vaguely disappointed, though she had no reason to be, that he wasn't coming in again. "Thanks for the wallet. You didn't have to."

He stood unmoving for a moment, his expression grown serious, before he said, "You're welcome."

Still he made no move to go. Marjo trained her eyes on his shirt collar, acutely aware of the silence between them, the soft evening sounds around them, the fading, pink-tinted light. Her breath quickened as she sensed him studying her face. She dropped her gaze to the ground between them, uncertain of his intention, equally uncertain of her own wishes.

"I know you're not looking for anything serious. I guess you have your reasons," he said softly. "But I want to say . . . Oh, hell. This is what I want to do . . ."

His hand tipped her chin up, and his mouth touched hers—warm, soft, tasting of Opie's cake. His strong arms wrapped around her back and pulled her briefly against him. She felt the soft thud of his heartbeats against her chest, then he released her, his mouth lingering a moment after his arms let her go, as if testing her willingness to return the kiss.

He lifted his head, and his gaze rested on her mouth for a moment, then he met her startled eyes and gave her a slow, easy smile. "See you Friday, Ms. Opaski."

He turned, walked toward the corner, and was out of sight. She heard the car door slam and the engine start, then the crunch of tires on gravel as he drove out of her parking lot, and she was left alone with the soft evening breeze, the darkening sunset, and the first twinkling stars.

With a deep, shaky breath, she pulled open her front door and went in.

CHAPTER THREE

"MOM. THEY'RE HERE."

Marjo glanced up from the dish of dog food in her hands. "Who?"

"*Them*. You know—Flash and Mr. What's-his-name."

Marjo nodded, enlightened. "Oh." She went back to the dog food, refraining from further comment. Opie had been unable to remember Matt Rutgers' name since his visit Tuesday evening.

"You better hide your wallet."

"I think the wallet's safe, Opie."

"They've got someone with them, too. Some dopey-looking kid with glasses."

She set the dish of dog food in Dicey's kennel and shut the gate. "That's not a particularly nice way to describe someone, Opie."

The girl made a face. "Okay. Some skinny, short kid with dirty-blond hair and a kind of squashed-up nose and a yucky sweater. With glasses."

"Thanks, Opie. That's a lot better." She gave her daughter a wry glance. "It's probably Mr. Rutgers' son —Timmy."

"Figures." Opie marched out, her stiff spine expressing a definite opinion about Timmy.

Marjo took a breath, then winced as the door slammed. Apparently, her daughter had decided Matt Rutgers was a threat.

It was an attitude Marjo had encountered before, though she'd never had to take it seriously; the simple truth was that the few men she'd dated since she'd been free of her marriage had never constituted any kind of threat. They'd been—all three of them—responsible, mature businessmen, and the relationships had been casual, shallow, and short. None of them had made her stomach flutter or her heartbeat quicken, or caused that unnerving pulse of physical attraction that made her remember she was a woman first, a businesswoman second.

She hesitated at the door to take another deep breath before she reached for the doorknob.

Matt Rutgers was a *client,* she reminded herself, as she wiped her palms on her jeans. He'd probably forgotten all about that brief parting kiss. She'd do well to forget about it herself. What she didn't need in her ordered life—ordered with care and good sense—was a fling with some overconfident, irresponsible *client,* for heaven's sake. She was too old, and too wise, to fall for a practiced flirt like Matt Rutgers. No matter how good-looking he was. Or how well he kissed.

Or what he did to her palms.

She pulled open the door and strode out to the yard.

The little group of three at the corner of the kennel runs was impossible to miss. The dog strained toward the kennels, at the end of his leash, while Matt pulled back on the other end, muttering ineffective commands, and a young boy in glasses looked on. The scene was enough to bring a shudder to the most jaded of dog trainers.

Flash caught sight of Marjo as she approached and lunged toward her. The leash slipped through Matt's unprepared fingers, and the dog charged across the yard, ears flapping, tail wagging in joyous greeting, and leaped for Marjo's chest. She sidestepped, grabbed for the leash, and brought her knee up. It met Flash's midsection, throwing him off balance just as she pulled up the leash and brought the dog neatly to a sitting position. "Sit!" she commanded.

The dog sat, looking a little bewildered.

Matt Rutgers watched in surprise. "Godda—" He glanced at the boy beside him and cut off the expression. "Ms. Opaski," he amended.

"Mr. Rutgers."

The familiar grin, pleased, easygoing, slightly crooked, widened in flattering admiration. Matt Rutgers' gaze drifted down over her pale yellow sweat shirt, pausing long enough to read the message on the front of it: IF YOU CAN'T TAKE THE FLEAS, STAY OUT OF THE KENNEL, and continued down the length of her jean-clad legs, then drifted back up. It lingered for a moment on her mouth before he met her eyes.

He hadn't, it seemed, forgotten the kiss. She wiped her hands again on her jeans, then shifted her flustered gaze to the boy beside his father. "You must be Timmy," she greeted him.

The boy nodded, and Matt smiled at him. "This is Ms. Opaski, Tim."

"How do you do?" Timmy murmured. He held out his hand politely, and Marjo shook it. His light brown hair was neatly trimmed and clean, and he wore a tan cotton designer sweater. His nose, despite Opie's description, looked normal.

"I thought Timmy might join us for Friday lessons, if that's all right with you," Matt said to Marjo.

"Oh, yes. That's fine."

"I've told him what we learned in the last lesson. He wants to work with Flash at home. These two are great pals." He grinned down at the dog as Timmy reached out to scratch the hound's ears. Then Matt turned his crooked, likable grin toward Marjo.

Good grief. How could such an inept dog owner be so sexy? She jammed her hands into her pockets, smiled in self-defense, and took refuge in practiced professional euphemism. "Shall we start with a little review?"

"Sure."

"Why don't you walk him at heel for a few yards, then turn and come back? In that direction," she added hastily, gesturing away from the kennels. "One sharp tug."

Matt nodded, his gaze on her face, looking as if he were not listening with particular attention. "Right."

She handed him the leash, and he took his time gathering it into his left hand, in the meantime letting his gaze linger on her face before he leaned over and gave the dog a quick pat. "Okay, boy. Heel."

The two started off at a walk, the dog glancing up at Matt in evident obedience, keeping sedately within range of the shortened leash. Matt stopped after a few paces and turned back toward Marjo and Timmy, an expression of pleased, somewhat surprised satisfaction on his face.

"Heel!" he commanded again. Matt looked up at Marjo, lifted his hand in an "OK" sign, thumb and forefinger touching, and ignored the dog. Flash charged forward, toward the kennels, hauling on the leash and towing Matt behind him before the surprised would-be trainer realized what was happening.

"Hey! Flash, heel! Come on, boy—heel!" Matt pulled back on the leash, tightening the collar around the dog's neck and trying ineffectively to drag him back to position, as he was propelled foot by foot toward the kennels.

Marjo stepped neatly in front of them to cut off Flash's route, and the two of them came to an untidy halt.

"Dad," Timmy pointed out, "you're choking him."

Matt's disgruntled gaze moved from his son to Marjo in protest.

"One sharp tug," she told him.

"Right," he muttered.

It was clear from the next try that Matt had lost the hang of it. Flash towed his master across the yard and back again, the dog's tongue lolling out, his breath coming in short gasps as the training collar cut off his wind. Marjo gritted her teeth, watched in silence, and willed herself to exercise diplomacy.

"Dad," Timmy said again, a note of accusation in his voice, "you're still choking him."

Matt held out one hand, palm up, in a gesture of exasperation. "I'm not trying to choke him, Tim—but the darned animal has a mind of his own! He just doesn't seem to *want* to heel." He looked to Marjo for support. She glanced away politely and ran a finger under the collar of her sweat shirt in silent comment.

"Dad, maybe you should let me try."

"Well, I don't know, Tim—"

"I think I could do it, Dad. Come on."

"Tim, this dog is awfully strong." He glanced from Tim's hopeful face to Marjo's, his own expression doubtful.

Marjo's speculative gaze moved from father to son, then to the dog. Flash outweighed Tim by at least twenty pounds, but it wasn't size and strength that made a good dog trainer. She glanced back to Matt, whose impressive strength and fully developed physique gave ample proof of that truism. Tim could hardly do worse than his father. She turned her eyes away from Matt's impressive physique and commented, "I don't think it would hurt to let Timmy try."

Matt looked doubtfully from the dog to his son, but Timmy nodded with businesslike determination as he took the leash. His face set, he looped up the slack in the leash, then commanded, "Heel!", and set off.

Flash walked at heel for a few paces, then his ears pricked up at some sound across the yard, and he charged ahead. Unlike his father, Tim was prepared for the charge. He dropped the loop, let the dog reach the end of the slack, then threw himself back against it, hanging on to the leash with both hands. Flash came to a sharp, skidding stop. Timmy was yanked off his feet to sail in a smooth, improbable arc through the air. He hit the gravel elbows first, with a grunt and a crunch of small stones.

"Oh, my God—" Matt dashed toward his son, Marjo a step behind him, but Tim had already picked himself up, gathered up the leash, and ordered, "Heel!" with more authority than Marjo had heard since she'd consulted in a class for police dogs.

Flash glanced up at his young trainer, panted once, and walked at heel, obviously convinced that Timmy meant business. By the time the boy had completed a circle of the yard, Flash was heeling perfectly, and Tim was smiling with pleasure.

The grin on Matt's face almost matched the one on his son's. "Hey! Way to go, Tim!" He turned to Marjo. "Look at that! He's doing a great job, isn't he?"

"Yes. He's doing just fine."

"Look at him! He's a natural."

His enthusiasm was infectious, and, watching him, Marjo chuckled appreciatively. Matt stood with feet widespread, hands thrust deep into the pockets of his chinos, broad shoulders hunched slightly as he leaned forward to follow Timmy's progress across the yard. He beamed with excited interest, his pride in his son genuine and wholehearted, completely undimmed, it seemed, by the fact that Matt himself had just failed miserably at the same task.

Involuntarily making a comparison, Marjo tried to

picture her ex-husband showing the same enthusiasm about something Opie had acomplished. The image wouldn't come. Stan's ego wouldn't have withstood the unflattering comparison of his own abilities to those of a child.

Yet the father's pride did nothing to detract from this man's masculinity, she noted with a catch in her breath. On the contrary, it added to his virile appeal in a way she found hard to ignore.

Matt glanced toward her and met her eyes, his own gaze open, pleased, willing her to share his pleasure, and she felt her heart lurch into a higher gear. Then he turned back to the boy and the dog, leaving Marjo groping, again, for reasons to mistrust him, and coming up with a disturbingly short list.

By the end of the lesson, Timmy was doing so well that Marjo had him move on to the command "Sit!", showing him the straight, palm-raised hand signal and backward tug on the leash to give Flash the message.

They had gone considerably over their half hour when Marjo glanced at her watch, then looked up to see Opie standing at the corner of the grooming shed, observing the lesson. With elaborately casual interest, the girl wandered toward them to get a closer look. Timmy brought the dog back, keeping him at his left heel, then ordered, "Sit!", and gave the hand signal Marjo had shown him. Flash sat, without further prompting, and Timmy looked up with a pleased, prideful grin. The boy's forehead was streaked with dirt, his hair dusty and disheveled from his fall. He had a scrape on one hand, and his tan sweater had holes in both elbows and bits of gravel clinging to the front.

Opie surveyed him up and down, her mouth quirked thoughtfully. She nodded slightly, apparently finding his appearance an improvement. "You're doing pretty good," she told him in grudging praise.

"Thanks." He ducked his head to scratch the dog's long ears.

"Opie, this is my son, Timmy," Matt said. "Tim—Opie."

The boy nodded once, hesitated as if wondering how to acknowledge the introduction, then muttered, "How d'you do," and held out his hand.

Opie stared at it, then shook hands with him, frowning, and stuck her own hands back into her pockets, obviously unwilling to go so far as to be friends. The moment threatened to stretch out into awkward silence, but Matt put in, with a judicious amount of casual admiration, "Opie bakes a mean cake, Tim. I had a piece the other night—it was delicious. Four layers."

"Oh, gee." Tim looked up. "I made a cake for Dad's birthday. It was only two layers, though. And it was a little burned around the edges."

Opie regarded Tim with unsmiling seriousness. "You probably had the oven too hot."

"Yeah, maybe."

"That could have been it, huh?" Matt asked, his gaze interested, open to advice, engagingly willing to be instructed by a ten-year-old expert.

Opie shrugged, and her mouth tipped up in the suggestion of a smile. "Sure."

"Maybe someday you'll show us how to make the four-layer concoction, Opie."

The girl shrugged again, her smile now slightly superior and infinitely more gracious. "I'd be happy to give you the recipe. I think it would take a little practice, though, to get it right."

"We'd like that, Opie. And you could give us some tips on the practice." Matt grinned at her, and Marjo watched her daughter preen in the light of that charming, crooked, sincere grin, while the name Matt Rutgers was miraculously restored to Opie's memory, and her resistance to Timmy faded into unimportance. The Opaski women, it seemed, were universally susceptible.

"Well—" Matt turned his grin toward Marjo, and she felt her pulse quicken in predictable but no less disarming response to the warmth in those brown eyes. "I appreciate the extra time you've given us," he said.

"No problem."

"We've probably made you late for dinner, though."

"It's all right."

"Tell you what. Why don't I take us all out for pizza?"

"Oh, no—that's not—"

"South Shore Pizza House has great food. You like pizza?" he addressed Opie.

"Dinner's no problem, really," Marjo put in.

"Tim likes the place because they have great video games. You like video games, Opie?"

Opie's interest had been thoroughly caught. She shifted her weight to one foot, ever-so-smoothly looped her hair behind one ear, and said, "Yes, I like them."

"I don't know," Marjo said again. "Opie and I had some plans for dinner—"

"We could do that tomorrow, Mom."

"Fine," Matt put in. "We may as well all go in my car. The dog can stay in the back. There's room for everyone."

He glanced at Marjo, waiting for her reply, his expression guileless and inviting. His engagingly crooked smile flashed toward her, and she felt her defenses wobble like oak leaves in October. "I—uh—I'm really not dressed for going out," she muttered lamely.

His brown eyes, with those devilish glints, slid down over the saying on the front of her sweat shirt, snug, faded jeans, blue rubber duck shoes, then made a leisurely journey back up to her face. It was tinted a delicate pink when he got to it.

Again he flashed her that crooked smile. "You look great," he said, softly enough to make it personal.

Twenty minutes later, they pulled into the crowded parking lot of a small pizza house that boasted universal suburban decor and the delicious smell of garlic and tomato sauce.

"You wait here for us, Flash," Timmy instructed as they all got out of the car. There was a brief silence after the slamming of the car doors, then a mournful, carrying howl emanated from the back of the station wagon as Flash realized he was being abandoned.

"Oh, dear." Marjo stopped walking and half turned back to the car.

Matt caught her elbow and gently guided her toward the pizza house. "Pretend you don't hear it."

"Pretend we don't hear it? How could we not hear it? He sounds like the hound of the Baskervilles."

Another bansheelike howl filled the parking lot. Opie made a face and looked back over her shoulder. "He sounds like he's having his toenails pulled out," she offered descriptively.

"Yeah. And his ears cut off," Timmy added.

"I know what he sounds like," Matt said, walking toward the door. "I listen to him daily."

"He does this every day?" Marjo asked, incredulous.

"Uh-huh. He'll stop after fifteen minutes or so. Just pretend you don't know him."

Marjo shot Matt a skeptical look but let him guide her into the pizza house. The howls were clearly audible even after the door had shut behind them.

"Maybe we should quiet him down, Matt."

"How?" He turned toward her, hands outspread, expression resigned.

"Well . . ." She had to concede that she didn't have any ideas. The parking lot of a pizza house wasn't the ideal place for dog training.

"We'll just pretend we don't hear him."

"But..." Marjo glanced around at the restaurant's clientele, then smiled nervously and followed Matt to the counter to order pizza.

"What'll you have, kids?" Matt queried.

"Pepperoni," Timmy answered.

Opie gave him an assessing look, then nodded in approval. "With mushrooms," she added.

"Pepperoni with mushrooms?"

Flash howled again.

"Yes," Marjo said, cringing slightly, "pepperoni with mushrooms is fine."

Matt turned an insouciant grin toward the waitress at the counter, who looked up to take their order.

"Two pepperoni with mushrooms, large," he said, "and two Cokes, and"—he glanced at Marjo—"what will you have to drink? Beer?"

The call of the wild drifted in from the parking lot, escalating to a pitch of intensity and mournfulness that was impressive in its dramatic impact.

"Beer, yes," Marjo muttered.

The girl at the counter tipped her head, listening, a wary expression on her face.

"And two beers," Matt told her.

Flash howled again.

The girl glanced over her shoulder nervously, obviously disconcerted by the unearthly sounds outside.

"Wolves," Matt told her seriously. "I've heard they're making a comeback in Milwaukee."

She stared back at him, suspicion replacing the confusion on her face.

"Sounds like a dominant female to me," Matt went on, glancing at Marjo.

She gave him a strained smile in return. "I'd say it sounds more like an out-of-line male."

The girl at the counter looked from one to the other,

then smiled weakly, humoring them, and muttered, "Two beers."

"Right."

Matt picked up the beers and shepherded them all to a booth near the video games, where the sounds from the parking lot were overpowered by the noise of the machines. Opie and Tim collected fifty cents each from their parents and went off together, and Marjo looked after them, watching them a little longer than was natural, keenly conscious of Matt Rutgers sitting across from her at the booth. She linked her hands around her mug of beer and stared into it, suddenly at a loss for words.

"I have a feeling they'll get along fine," Matt said. "Opie seems to have decided Timmy's okay."

She looked up to catch his serious brown eyes studying her from across the table. The solemn expression, and the evidence of understanding that went with it, was unnerving. What she expected from Matt Rutgers was light banter and irreverent flirtation. That she could handle, could resist. But the occasional glimpse of a thoughtful, sensitive man behind the good-natured humor was more than she wanted to consider.

She looked down again. Silence fell between them as Matt sipped his beer and Marjo stared into hers. She could think of nothing to say. She couldn't remember the last time she'd been out for pizza with a man.

It had been years since she and Opie had been out together with Stan, and even those occasions had been few and far between. There'd never been enough extra money for luxuries like a family night out.

A warning vibrated in the center of her chest, evoked by this situation, with its trappings of a past she'd never had: family outings, Mom and Dad sitting together while the kids played video games and the family dog howled out in the car.

What was she doing, longing after a fantasy that

didn't exist outside of TV sitcoms and the daydreams of single working mothers like herself, who should know better? And who *should* have known better, she chided herself, than to be talked into coming here with Matt Rutgers and feeling awkward and unschooled and out of her element.

Matt set his beer on the table, assessing her downcast gaze, stiff shoulders, and small hands with their short, unpolished nails toying with the untouched beer. "Would you rather have a Coke?" he asked her.

She looked up, startled out of her morose thoughts, and shook her head. "Oh, no. Beer's fine." She gave him a slight, perfunctory smile. "You don't grow up in Milwaukee without learning to drink beer."

"Did you? Grow up in Milwaukee?"

"Yes." She nodded slightly, then gave him another stiff smile. "Well, Racine, actually. Not far from where I am now."

"Do your folks still live here?"

"No. They're retired. They have a year-round camp on Lake Koshkonong." She looked down again, then glanced back toward the video machines, where garish lights and technological sound effects were keeping a dozen youngsters entertained.

"They're probably playing Pole Position, if Timmy has anything to say about it," Matt commented.

She turned back, looking self-conscious, her hands still toying nervously with her mug.

Matt sipped his beer again, watching her through narrowed eyes, then the corners of his mouth turned up in a grin. "I can't figure out if you're worried about Opie—or about me."

Two blotches of becoming color appeared in her face. "No—it's just that I've—I mean—I've never been here before." She picked up her mug of beer, holding it in front of her as if she needed a barrier between them. "Do you—come here a lot?"

"Mmm." He nodded. "Some of my students brought me here a couple of years ago." He grinned. "They claimed it was for the pizza, but I think they just wanted to beat the pants off me at the video games."

She smiled a little more naturally. "And did they?"

"Yup." He chuckled. "Every last one of them. It was my first year of teaching. They weren't college-track kids, but I was convinced they could learn physics, and I'd been pushing them all year to make them do it. I think they wanted to show me there was a place where they could outshine me."

"Oh." She paused. "I didn't know teachers went out for pizza with their students."

He shrugged. "Sometimes what you give kids out of class is more important than what you can teach them from a book."

Her blue eyes thoughtful, Marjo set down her beer. "Sounds like you like your job."

"I do. It's given me more satisfaction than anything else I've done."

She looked mildly surprised. "You haven't always been a teacher?"

"No. I trained as an engineer."

"An engineer? You mean bridges and things?"

"No, hydraulics. I designed automobile transmissions."

"Oh." She colored again—attractively—at her mistake, but went on. "And you just . . . quit, to go into teaching?"

"Well, it wasn't exactly that simple." He scanned her face, wondering how much to say, then shrugged and stated equably, "It was hard for Anne to accept. She married an up-and-coming engineer who suddenly decided to chuck it for half the income and none of the status."

"Oh." There was another pause. "I guess—that must have made it hard for you, too."

"Mmm. It's hard on everyone when a marriage breaks up. And career changes are hard on marriages. You probably know that as well as I do."

She gave a self-deprecating laugh, looking down again. "I wouldn't know about careers. I barely finished high school. I was six months pregnant when I got my degree."

His gaze rested on her for a moment, then he said quietly, "I know how tough that is. I admire you for sticking it out until you finished."

She shot him a quick, furtive look through long lashes, then dropped her gaze.

"Also," he added, "for everything else you've accomplished."

"Oh . . ." She gave him a fleeting, self-conscious smile and picked up her beer again.

To hide behind, he thought wryly. "Hey"—he set his own mug on the table, reached in his pocket for change, then tipped his head toward the video machines—"want to play?"

She glanced up, caught off guard. "You mean the videos?"

"Sure." He smiled.

"But I, uh, I don't know how."

"I'll show you." He shrugged, scooting over in the booth. "Come on. It's fun."

She hesitated for a moment, then slid out of the booth and followed him.

They wandered past several machines flashing gaudy images of star wars, western scenery, and improbable life-forms, then Matt stopped in front of one labeled POLE POSITION. Graphics of a racetrack were displayed on the screen, and the machine had a steering wheel, instead of the usual joy stick. He fed two quarters into the slot and pushed the start button. ONE DRIVER, flashed onto the screen. PUSH ACCELERATION PEDAL TO BEGIN.

Marjo was frowning skeptically at the display. "Want to go first?" he asked her.

She shook her head. "I don't know what to do."

"Just pretend you're driving. You have to keep the car on the track. Here." He stepped back, grasped her shoulders from behind, and moved her in front of the screen. "Pretend you're in a silver Porsche with black leather interior and every amenity you've ever wanted."

She let out a little chuckle. "But I never wanted a Porsche."

"A Ferrari, then. Or a DeLorean. What'll it be, Ms. Opaski?"

"I . . . don't know." She rested her hands experimentally on the black plastic steering wheel. "Where's the acceleration pedal?"

"Uh-uh. You have to decide what kind of car it is, first."

But . . ." She gave him a bemused glance. "Your fifty cents will run out."

"Naw, not yet." He grinned at her. "And anyway, what's fifty cents for the sports car of your dreams?"

"Well, then . . ." She stared at the screen, glanced back at Matt, then finally shrugged, palms widespread in front of her. "I don't dream about sports cars. I could never afford a sports car . . ."

Matt Rutgers assessed her, his gaze perceptive. The freckles across her nose made her look young, unsophisticated, vulnerable. Like the teenager she'd been when her chance for sports cars and rock concerts and all the other trappings that should go with that stage of life had been abruptly eliminated, by the same sudden initiation into adulthood that had happened to some of his own students.

The kind of adulthood that came with teenage pregnancy, he knew, was pretty stark. Facing it and making something of it took grit and determination—and too much hard work. He studied Marjo's expression, then his lips curved in a slight smile. "Dream a little bit, Ms. Opaski. I'm buying."

The long lashes dropped down over her gaze. She turned back toward the screen, then shrugged again. "Well . . . a Corvette, I guess."

"What color?"

She took a breath and stared upward for a moment. "Ice blue. With beige interior."

"Beige?"

She glanced at him again. "Well, maybe red."

He nodded approval. "Okay. Go for it, Ms. Opaski."

She stepped on the pedal. A sports car appeared on the screen, traveling along a road that curved suddenly to the right. She spun the steering wheel a fraction of a second too late, and the car crashed into the side of the road with a splash of video graphics. "Good grief," she muttered. Matt chuckled behind her.

A new car appeared on the screen, and Marjo stepped on the acceleration pedal again. The car followed the road for a second or two, then crashed into a bridge abutment that had suddenly appeared on the screen. Marjo made a sound of exasperation, gripped the steering wheel harder, and looked determinedly at the screen as the next car appeared. But the graphics display was geared to highly experienced preteens, and Marjo's car crashed into an oncoming car. The game just as quickly disposed of Marjo's next try. The screen blanked out, and the words FINISHED: SCORE: 17, appeared in front of her.

"Oh!" She clicked her tongue in disappointment, then gave a huff of philosophical laughter. "Well, I told you I didn't know anything about sports cars."

He produced another fifty cents and dropped the money into the coin slot. "Try again."

"Oh, I don't think I'm very good at this."

"I'll help you." He reached around her and covered her hands on the steering wheel, then leaned down, his head close to hers, to peer at the screen. She turned her head and gave him a disconcerted glance. He grinned back at her and moved a little closer. "Come on, Ms. Opaski. Time's running out."

The message, PUSH ACCELERATON PEDAL TO BEGIN, was flashing on the screen insistently.

"Mmm. I like this car," Matt muttered into her ear. He wiggled the steering wheel. "Nice feel to it."

Her shoulder blades touched the front of his chest, the muscles of her back stiff and unyielding. The small hands under his fingers on the plastic steering wheel gave a hesitant tug away. He tightened his hold.

"We need some acceleration, Ms. Opaski," he prompted.

She gave a small, breathy laugh, the corners of her mouth turned up in a half-smile, and stopped tugging. "All right, all right. Acceleration," she grumbled good-naturedly as she stepped on the pedal. A car appeared on the video roadway.

"Okay," Matt said into her ear. "Left, now . . . all right. No! Watch it! Watch it!" He spun the steering wheel hard to the right. His arm pressed against her shoulder as the car crashed on the screen, and he let out a whoosh of breath that fanned the hair at the side of her face and made her glance at him again, her blue eyes wide with an awareness that he could feel all the way to his toes.

"Okay. Try once more." He moved in closer, resting his cheek against her temple. Her hair smelled of floral shampoo. Her elbows brushed the inside of his arms as she relaxed a little against him. Electricity traveled down Matt's body to where her body brushed the front of his chinos.

She let out a low chuckle and complained, "You're not much help, Mr. Rutgers," but her voice had a dis-quietingly husky note, and from the pulse at the side of

her neck, he could tell her heart was thudding in a
giddy, erratic rhythm.

"Come on. Let's go, Ms. Opaski."

"We're acting like . . . kids," she told him, her voice
flustered.

"Mmm," he agreed, brushing the palms of his hands
against her knuckles.

She stepped on the pedal again.

This time, they managed to make it around two
curves before they crashed the car. FINISHED: SCORE: 68
was the message that flashed in front of them.

"I think we're getting the hang of it," Matt commented. He released one of her hands to fish in his
pocket for more quarters, but came up with only dimes
and nickels. He jingled the change, staring into his palm
as if quarters would magically appear while he stood
with one arm around her in front of the video machine,
then he grinned down at her. "Got any quarters, Ms.
Opaski?"

From the counter, a waitress called out, "Number
fifty-six!"

"That's our number, isn't it?" she asked.

"Is it?" His voice fell as he shot a distracted glance
toward the counter; then he looked back at Marjo.

"I think so." Her voice was breathy, and the level of
disturbance it revealed held a promise that was almost
—*almost*—he thought wryly, worth the interruption.

He replaced the change in his pocket, taking his
time. His chest rose and fell with a slow, pensive
breath, then he let go of her hand. "I think maybe that
is our number, Ms. Opaski," he repeated, grinning at
her.

CHAPTER FOUR

MATT CLAIMED THEIR order and rounded up Tim and Opie, then slid in beside Marjo when he returned to the booth, leaving the opposite seat for the two children. His grin was casual, his attention ostensibly on Opie and Tim as the youngsters joined them, but he slid over on the seat until his shoulder touched Marjo's and his forearm skimmed her sleeve as he pushed the first pizza toward the center of the table. "Eat up, kids." Under the table, Matt's thigh brushed against hers.

Tim opened the pizza carton and helped himself to the first piece. "How'd you do, Dad?" he asked.

"Sixty-eight," Matt reported solemnly.

"Dad . . ." Tim shook his head, an expression on his face that reminded Marjo of his father: mock-serious-ness with a glint in his eye, "that's not very good."

"We had a good time, though." Matt slanted a side-ways look at Marjo and grinned. Her pulse skipped a beat, and she drew in a quick, unconscious breath.

Tim grinned back, but Opie cast Matt a silent look of appraisal before her curious gaze moved to her mother. Marjo's slight smile wasn't returned. Instead, Opie studied her with dawning suspicion.

A moment later, the girl picked up her Coke and reached for a slice of pizza, but Opie's mood cast a dampening silence over the meal, and made Marjo all the more aware, by contrast, of the sensual tension that fluttered in her midsection and tingled at the side of her hip, where it pressed against Matt's jeans.

She moved discreetly away from him on the seat, and made an attempt at natural conversation with her daughter and Timmy, but she was attuned to Matt's presence with every atom of her body, and her reaction to him made her feel as though she were a living neon sign illustrating "sexual attraction" to the curious and censorious eyes of her ten-year-old daughter.

Marjo felt relieved when they finally finished the pizza, paid the bill, and walked out to the car.

The abandoned dog came to life as Opie and Tim got into the back seat. Flash whimpered and panted his greetings, drooling happily on the upholstery as both children scratched his ears and reassured him that he'd been missed.

Matt reached in front of Marjo to open the car door for her, then held it as she got in. The small courtesy surprised her into an unguarded glance at his face, her blue eyes wide and a little uncertain in the dim light of the parking lot. "Thanks," she muttered almost inaudibly.

He smiled at her. "My pleasure."

She smiled back nervously, aware that the pleasure wasn't entirely his. Not by a long shot.

There was little conversation in the car on the ride back. Even as incorrigible a flirt as Matt Rutgers had to act sedate when there were two ten-year-old chaperons in the back seat, one of them transmitting disapproval that was hard to ignore. And for that, she told herself, she was grateful. It was a reprieve from feelings that were moving too fast from temptations she hadn't felt since she'd been in high school, when Stan had been the best-looking, most exciting boy she'd ever met, and she'd had no idea how to deal with the overwhelming, exciting feelings he evoked in her. She shot a covert glance at Matt, wondering with a swift, nervous shiver of alarm if she had any better idea how to deal with them now.

Matt whistled snatches of an old, vaguely familiar tune as he drove them home through a quiet residential neighborhood of square stone houses and wide lawns.

Three blocks later, she identified the tune and glanced toward him sharply as her memory filled in the well-known, romantic words about lovers and spring-time.

Good grief. With two kids and a dog in the back seat of his station wagon, he'd found a way to flirt with her. She almost smiled, in spite of her misgivings. He stared innocently ahead of him, lips pursed, casually filling her brain with romantic lyrics. Fighting the tendency of her mouth to curve up at the corners, she stared out the window, ignoring him.

He went on whistling lyrics about the magic of a kiss.

Marjo resolutely watched south Milwaukee pass by and made an effort not to think about kissing Matt Rutgers.

The kennels were dark, the lot empty, as they pulled into a parking space in front of Marjo's house. Matt was out of the car and around to her side of it before she could offer a quick, casual good night. He draped his arm around her shoulders and walked her toward her front door. Marjo kept her hands in her pockets, willing herself to ignore the weight of his arm, the brush of his thigh against hers, conscious of Opie and Tim behind them. But it was impossible to forget that he had kissed her here a few days ago. Song lyrics stubbornly re-peated themselves in her imagination.

He stopped at the door, casually swinging around toward the kids. "Tim, why don't you have Opie show you the kennels?"

Opie's mouth dropped open in protest.

Ill-at-ease with Opie's suspicious glare, Marjo moved away from the circle of Matt's arm. He dropped it to his side with a glance in her direction.

"What's that supposed to mean?" Opie blurted out. "You two want to be *alone* or something?"

Matt gave her a level look, then nodded. "That's the general idea, yes."

"Oh, I see." Opie gave the words a distinctly dramatic flare. "Well, I know when I'm not *wanted* . . ." She stalked off in the direction of the kennels, Tim following a few paces behind.

"Opie—"

But she rounded the corner, ignoring her mother.

Matt's glance followed the two children. "Kids!" he stated, shaking his head with mock disgust. "It's a good thing they're lovable." He turned back to Marjo, a wry grin on his lips, but the expression faded as he met her troubled look.

She sketched an unconvincing smile, then dropped her gaze to her hands. "Listen, Matt"—she laced her fingers together self-consciously—"Opie is . . ."

"Hey . . ." He smiled again and gave a slight shrug. "Her reaction is pretty normal. I guess it's just human nature not to want any competition for the people we love. But kids can—"

"Opie's not just *any* kid!"

He studied her a moment, his expression bemused at her vehemence. "No, of course not," he said finally, softly. "She's a great little girl. Some day soon, she'll be a fine young woman."

The serious, quietly spoken words brought a sudden, unforeseen tightening of her throat. Marjo pulled her gaze away from Matt's, staring at her white clapboard house as if expecting it to give her a way to put words to her feelings.

Matt said into the silence, "Look, I thought things went fine tonight. Tim and Opie got along better than anyone would have predicted. I thought we were having a good time—"

"We were. But—" She stared at her hands. "You don't understand."

"No," he said after a moment. "I guess I don't. Why don't you explain it to me?"

"It's . . . a long story."

He stood unmoving, unsmiling, in the gathering darkness of the spring evening, watching her and waiting.

She glanced up, finally, and took a breath. "Opie's had . . . a pretty rough childhood. Her father was—well—he couldn't handle the responsibility of a family."

She shrugged, and her voice grew hard, with a brittle edge that was sharply at odds with her usual manner. "Not for very long at one time, anyway. A few months was usually all he could manage before he'd disappear. He waltzed in and out of our lives like—like the flu." She smiled, but the expression was tight and unnatural.

"He'd walk out on us—leave us with all the bill collectors and the complaining landlord and no money and no decent-paying job—" She let out a cynical breath. "He didn't think his wife should work. So when he disappeared, I'd have to take the first job I could find, no matter what it was—and then we'd just about get our feet on the ground and he'd be back again. And he'd want me to quit my job and move to a new apartment and let him support us—until the next time he decided it was all *just too much* for him, and he'd take off again—"

Her fingers twisted together as she stared down at her hands. Matt was silent, listening to her. "Opie thought the sun rose and set on him," she said, her voice bitter. "Every time he came back he'd bring her presents— take her places—promise that he was back to stay. And every time he left, it was harder on her." She stared at Matt defiantly, eyes a little too bright, shoulders hunched as if for protection. "It took me seven years to dredge up enough self-respect to divorce him. I always thought if I tried hard enough—if I did enough things right—"

Matt was silent for a moment, then asked, "Is he still part of your lives?"

"No! And we don't want him as part of our lives, ever!"

The brown eyes assessed her defensive posture, the knotted hands, the revealing tremor in her voice. "Just you and Opie against the world, huh? Not going to let anyone else in?"

Her eyes flicked to his face again, and he stared back at her, studying her with sober understanding. Conflicting emotions swelled into a knot in her chest: guilt at brushing him off when he'd been nothing but hospitable to her and Opie; the instinctive, needful wish to trust him; guilty resentment that she should have to choose between her sense of self-preservation and her own human needs. She swallowed convulsively, trying to force down a bone-deep, terrifying longing for something she feared, for it had hurt her too many times to be trusted.

Slowly, Matt reached toward her, his fingers brushing a lock of blonde hair at her temple. "I hear what you're saying," he said softly, "about Opie. I know you want to protect her. But this counts, too." His hand circled her neck, his fingers threading into the hair at the back of her head. A current of electricity fanned out from his fingertips and quivered in her stomach as his mouth touched hers, gently, lightly. His free hand cupped the back of her head and tipped it up as he an-

gled his own head to fit their mouths together. She felt
the flick of his tongue along the edge of her lips, warm
and tantalizing; then, deliberately, he slid his hands
down over her shoulders and spread them wide on her
back, pressing her fully against him, letting her feel the
thud of his heart, the muscled length of his torso, the
hardness of his body where it pressed against her stomach.

Her fingers touched the sides of his jacket, clutched
at it briefly, then fluttered tentatively at his waist, neither encouraging nor resisting the kiss, but she knew he
could feel her own heart where it thrummed greedily in
her throat, and for a brief instant her lips opened to his
seeking tongue.

Too honorably for satisfaction, he pulled away from
her before the kiss grew more demanding. His hands
brushed up to her shoulders, and he massaged them a
little roughly as he stared down at her expression of
half-surprise, half-confusion.

"You'll see me again, Ms. Opaski," he said after a
moment, his beguiling mouth set in an even, determined
line. There wasn't a hint of question in his voice.

He gave her a nod, turned on his heel, and walked
toward the kennels. Marjo watched his retreating back,
trying to sort out her confusing mix of thoughts. As she
pulled open her door and walked inside, she knew with
acute, painful, reawakened longing exactly what she
felt.

Her thoughts were no more at ease when Opie came
upstairs. Marjo bustled around the living room with
restless energy, fluffing pillows on the couch, picking
up a discarded sweater from the arm of a chair, purposefully straightening a stack of magazines that was a
quarter-inch off-center on the coffee table.

Opie stood in the doorway, her eyes following her
mother's agitated movements. Finally, Marjo glanced up

at her and took a deep, controlling breath. "This belongs in your room, Opie," she said briskly, holding out the sweater.

Opie took it but made no move toward her room, still watching her mother, her look faintly accusing. "Well," she commented after a moment. "Did you have enough time alone with Mr. Rutgers?"

Marjo's hand froze in the act of reaching for a glass that had been left on the bookshelf. She felt a flush of color stain her cheeks, and met her daughter's eyes with guarded caution. "We just wanted a little privacy, Opie. Just—" She broke off, with a slight, ineffectual gesture of one hand.

Opie tossed her hair out of her eyes. "What'd you want to talk about?"

"Nothing special. I wanted to thank him for taking us—"

"Did you kiss him good night?"

Marjo stared back at her daughter; then, in spite of herself, felt her gaze skitter off in unmistakable admission.

Dammit, she didn't deserve Opie's censure. But—*dammit!*—she felt guilty. Guilty and disloyal and confused, and inadequate as a parent, and utterly unable to explain her feelings to herself, much less to the defiant, transparently vulnerable ten-year-old standing in front of her, twisting her best sweater into an agonized knot.

"Opie, Mr. Rutgers and I aren't—we're not—" She struggled for an explanation that would offer Opie reassurance. "I've just met him. We're not . . . dating."

"You played that video game with him!"

Marjo's color deepened, but she pulled herself up straighter, holding the glass in front of her. "A video game is not a date."

"Well, you went out for pizza with him."

"We *all* went out for pizza! As a matter of fact—" She bit off the obvious retort that it had been Opie who'd decided they would go, took another deep breath, then gave Opie a forced smile. "Honey, I thought you *wanted* to go. We don't do that sort of thing very often. It's nice sometimes to go out for supper like—like other people do."

Opie's mouth quirked up briefly, the habits of cooperation and allegiance winning out for a moment. "Yeah, I s'pose," she conceded, but her expression remained wary and indefinably hurt, as though she'd been, in some way, betrayed.

Marjo's shoulders slumped. She looked down at the glass in her hands, staring into it with troubled intensity before meeting Opie's eyes again, trying another smile. There was no response. After a moment, still with no better idea how to handle Opie's concerns, she sighed, turned away, and walked toward the kitchen.

Opie's voice followed her. "I just don't want you to think you have to provide me with a father, or anything like that."

Marjo turned back, startled.

"I mean, I *have* a father."

"Opie, honey—" She shook her head, momentarily speechless.

"Maybe he doesn't see me every weekend, like Tim's father. But that doesn't mean I don't *have* one!"

A chill settled in Marjo's stomach. "Opie," she said carefully, "your father and I are divorced. We're never going to live together again. He's not part of this family anymore."

"Well, he's still my *father!*" Opie pounded her fists against her thighs in a childish, angry gesture, then brushed past her mother and dashed into her bedroom, slamming the door behind her.

Marjo stared after her, her throat tight with panic. Opie hadn't seen her father in three years. Long enough for her to have forgotten him, wasn't it? Opie couldn't expect him to come back into her life now. *Could she?*

Marjo touched a trembling hand to her mouth, shaken at the thought of what Opie might expect. For time and again Stan *had* come back after an absence of indeterminate length. He'd come back laden with presents and promises—oh, he'd always been so glib with his extravagant promises! Always so ready to win his daughter's trust—and so quick to use Opie as the reason for making yet another new start to their rocky marriage.

She swallowed a lump in her throat that threatened to choke her with a too-well-remembered sense of powerless anger. He'd always come back with a new job. One he'd been sure that he could stick to this time. And he'd always promised that things would be different, that he'd take care of them, that he'd always loved them. He'd known—oh, yes, he'd known—how to convince her.

Her eyes closed as if to block out the unwanted memories. He'd always called her "Jo-Jo" when he was trying to win her over. She'd come to hate the cute, juvenile nickname.

Her fingers tightened around the glass she was holding until her knuckles were white. And always— *always!*—it would end with Opie in tears, crying for Daddy, and Marjo left alone, with no money and no job, fighting not to let her daughter see the panic that threatened to overwhelm her, or the impotent, cold rage she felt because she had let him do this to them again.

Opie's closed door stared back at her in deaf unresponsiveness.

Damn Stan Wozniak for still having the power to hurt Opie! It wasn't fair! She flung out her arm, as if in denial, and the glass slid from her hand and crashed, shattering, against a kitchen cabinet. Marjo stared at the broken glass through a mist of emotions too complex to make sense of.

How could this be happening *now*, after three years?

Opie's bedroom door opened cautiously. "Mom?" The girl stood looking uncertainly at the broken glass.

Marjo swiped at her eyes with one hand. "It's—I just dropped a glass, honey. It's okay."

"Oh." Opie took a couple of steps toward her. "Well, I'll, uh, you want me to help you clean it up?"

"Oh—honey—" Marjo stepped around the broken glass to her daughter and wrapped her arms around her in a fierce, protective hug as she fought her own tears. Opie squeezed back, wordlessly, until Marjo released her, brushed a strand of hair out of Opie's face and gave the girl a tremulous smile. "We'll clean it up together, okay? I'll sweep up the glass, you hold the dustpan."

Opie regarded her in troubled silence. After a moment she nodded, biting her lip. "Okay, Mom."

Opie was unwilling to talk about either Matt Rutgers or her father in the days that followed. Worried about what her daughter might be thinking, but reluctant to bring up the subject of Opie's father when, she hoped, Opie may have already started to forget it, Marjo spent the weekend grimly tackling kennel chores. Sunday afternoon she'd taken on the task of cleaning the yard, and she and Opie were raking gravel around the kennels when a car pulled into the front lot. Marjo looked up from her rake, wondering if one of her Sunday afternoon students had forgotten something and come back for it. A car door slammed.

"Who's that, do you think?" Opie asked.

"I don't know."

Five seconds later, the howl of an abandoned bloodhound answered the question.

"Oh," Opie commented.

Marjo glanced at her silently, but Opie's face gave no clue to her thoughts. Marjo leaned her rake against the side of the house and started around the walkway.

Matt and Tim were at the end of the kennel runs,

scratching Dicey's ears through the wire mesh. Matt looked up and grinned as Marjo and Opie approached. "Hi," he said simply.

Something lighthearted, buoyant, and pleasurable tingled down Marjo's spine. The memory of his kiss brought a catch to her breath that, despite her unresolved feelings, she couldn't deny.

"Hi."

"Through with classes for the afternoon?"

"Yes." She nodded. "We were just doing some yard work."

His swift glance took in her jeans and yet another sweat shirt, this one black with a white whale printed on the front. He grinned at her. "Save the whales?" he inquired. "Or is it Moby Dick?"

"Oh, this." She glanced down at her sweat shirt, smiling a little, then looked back up at him. "I don't know. I never figured it out. It's just another sweat shirt I wear for working around the kennels."

He let his gaze drift over her again in leisurely appraisal that made her intensely aware of her old jeans, baggy sweat shirt, unadorned face, hair arranged by an afternoon of running her fingers through it.

"I like your style, Ms. Opaski."

Her smile faded. There was a tightening in her throat. "Thank you."

Silence stretched between them for a moment, broken by a howl from Matt's dog. Matt turned his head toward the sound, then glanced back at Marjo. "Wolves," he said, deadpan, but the familiar twinkle was in his eyes.

One corner of her mouth tipped up. "I hear they've been a problem in Milwaukee."

"Maybe we can learn to live with it, though." He smiled back at her, his eyes glinting with mischief, and Marjo felt another tingle in her stomach.

"We stopped by," he went on, "to see if we could

have a lesson on Sundays instead of Tuesdays. That way Tim could be at both lessons. He—uh—" He grinned at Tim. "He seems to have more of a knack for dog training than I do."

"I—don't think Sundays will be a problem. I'm through with the puppy classes by four-thirty. Any time after that would work out."

"Good." He made the word somehow express personal satisfaction.

Marjo felt color in her cheeks. Her voice, when she spoke, was breathy, with a catch in it. "Did you—want to start tonight?"

"No, next week will be fine. I know you're not ready for us right now."

She felt, irrationally, disappointed. But it was all too true, she thought. She wasn't ready for Matt Rutgers. "Okay, then. Next week."

"Good," he said again, more softly.

"Thanks, Mrs. Opaski," Tim chimed in. "I really appreciate it."

Flash howled again. Tim glanced at his father, who obviously intended to ignore the dog, and gave Opie a surreptitious, *can-you-believe-it* look, then muttered, "I'll go tell him to be quiet."

Matt nodded amiably, his eyes on Marjo. She returned the gaze with fascinated attention, telling herself to act normally, to remember what he was doing here, to treat him like another client, but for the life of her, she was unable to look away.

"I have something for you," he said. He pulled a small, gold-wrapped package from his pocket and held it out.

"But . . . what—?" She took it from his hand.

"Open it."

She hesitated, glancing at him again, wondering if she should accept the gift. Then, unable to resist her curiosity, she pulled off the red bow and unwrapped the paper. In the tiny box, on a bed of jeweler's cotton, was an ice-blue Hot Wheels Corvette, the inside seats painted bright red with what looked like nail polish.

She turned it over in her fingers, an involuntary, disbelieving smile on her face.

"Matt—I . . ." She fell silent, unable to think of anything to say.

"Dream a little," he told her. He gave her a crooked grin, then turned without a good-bye to walk back to the parking lot.

Marjo stood holding the toy car until Opie moved a step closer to her and peered over her shoulder at the Corvette. "What is it?" she asked.

Marjo held it out to her. "It's . . . sort of a joke, Opie. About the video game." She shrugged, then smiled uncomfortably at her daughter.

Opie glanced at her, then stared at the car for a moment, frowning. She turned back toward the kennels without comment, leaving Marjo to look from Matt's retreating back to Opie's, still unclear where she stood between the two of them.

Two days after his Sunday visit, Matt called Marjo, to thank her, he explained, for changing his lesson schedule. It was a flimsy excuse for a call, and Matt hesitated for a moment after he'd stated it, his fingers brushing idly over the phone on his kitchen counter, then asked, "Were you in the middle of something?"

Her voice smiled. "A Parcheesi tournament. But it's almost over. Opie's beating me, as usual."

"Oh . . . well, sorry to interrupt your defeat."

"Oh, it's okay. I can be defeated anytime. And I was happy to change the lesson. It's nice that Tim will be able to join us."

He snorted. "I think Tim's going to be the one running this project. He has better luck with it than I do."

Her warm chuckle vibrated on the line. "I think you have an attitude problem, Mr. Rutgers."

"Uh-uh. I have a dog with an attitude problem. I took him to his first ball game yesterday—"

"Ball game? Oh, you mean the team you coach."

"Right. I *thought* he'd be happier than tied up at the house. He howled all through it."

"Well, maybe he just hates softball."

"How could anyone hate softball? It's like hating baseball, for Pete's sake. It's un-American!" He paused. "You do like baseball, don't you?"

"Baseball?" She put on a posh Eastern accent. "You mean that game where grown men in striped suits try to hit some tiny little ball with a stick, then run around in circles and slide in the dirt and get all *covered* with mud?"

He chewed on his lip, gazed up at his kitchen ceiling, and pronounced, "The House Un-American Activities Committee will hear about this, Ms. Opaski."

"I'm not worried, Mr. Rutgers," she told him airily. "I'll just tell the Committee what place your team is in, and they'll throw you out of court."

"Oh, now, wait a minute—"

"That is if they don't haul you off to jail for slandering an upstanding American dog. He was probably howling in sympathy for your team."

"Upstanding American dog, is he? My team was winning!"

"Oh, dear." They laughed together for a moment, and Matt felt his smile lingering, picturing her standing in her kitchen holding the phone, her hair tousled as it had been when she'd been standing inside the span of his arms in front of the video machine. He wondered if she was remembering, too.

She cleared her throat. "Listen—thanks for the Corvette," she told him. The words caught a little.

"You're welcome." He smiled into the phone, his curiosity satisfied.

There was a brief silence. "Well . . ." He waited for her to mention her waiting game of Parcheesi, but heard only another, tantalizing silence.

"Well," Matt said again, finally, "tell Opie not to forget my recipe."

"Okay," she promised. Then, as if the mention of her daughter's name was a reminder of complications Matt would rather she ignored, she finished, "I'll see you Friday, then."

"Friday," he echoed. There was another silence before he added, more softly, "Good-bye."

" 'Bye."

The phone clicked, then the line hummed with a dial tone. Marjo listened to it for a full thirty seconds before she hung up the receiver, gently, and let out a breath.

She stood up and pushed her hands into her pockets, then wandered into the living room and leaned against the doorway for a moment, watching her daughter.

Opie glanced up, elbows propped beside the Parcheesi board, idly rattling the dice in one hand.

"My turn?" Marjo asked.

"Yup." Opie dropped the dice into a Parcheesi cup at her mother's place.

"That was Matt Rutgers," Marjo said. She pulled her hands out of her pockets as she crossed over to the game and sat on the floor beside the playing board. "He asked you not to forget to write out the recipe for the cake."

Opie shrugged one shoulder, but gave no other response, apparently indifferent.

Marjo watched her for a moment. "He—uh—called to thank me for changing the lesson so Tim could join in," she said.

Opie gave a flick of her head that indicated the barest minimal response and turned back pointedly to the game.

Marjo studied her a moment longer, then let out a sigh at Opie's unresponsiveness and picked up the dice. She rolled them out. "Umm." She groaned in mock disappointment. "Another three."

Opie glanced at her silently, then reached for the dice and shook them out. "Doubles," she stated in satisfaction.

Marjo sighed. "That probably does it, Ope. You win again."

"Yup." Opie pushed herself up to a sitting position, leaning back against the couch, then stared down at the round wooden players on the Parcheesi board, but made no move to advance them. Finally, she glanced up at her mother again. "Mom?"

"Yes?"

"I was thinking." Opie fiddled self-consciously with the Parcheesi men. "I haven't seen Gram and Grampa for a long time."

Expecting a comment about Matt, Marjo was taken aback by the change of subject. "But you saw them two weeks ago, Ope."

"No, I mean Gram and Grampa Wozniak."

Marjo frowned. It was unusual for Opie to ask to see Stan's parents, though they lived in the city and Marjo kept up a polite, if distant, relationship with them.

"I thought maybe I would call them."

"Well . . . of course. If you want to."

Opie set the dice holder down beside her. "I'd better do it now. While I think of it," she added.

Opie got to her feet and disappeared into the kitchen, then turned back suddenly in the doorway and stood looking at her mother, a doubtful expression on her face. "Is that . . . okay with you, Mom?"

Puzzled, Marjo repeated, "Yes—of course."

Opie went back into the kitchen, and her mother heard her dialing the phone. A moment later she reappeared in the doorway. "Can I stay overnight on Thursday?"

"A school night?"

"Gram says she'll drive me to school Friday morning. They're going away this weekend."

Marjo hesitated, again wondering about Opie's motives. Was she trying to reassure herself that she had a family, like "normal" kids? She felt a pang of irrational hurt that Opie didn't feel that her mother was family enough, but dismissed it, feeling ashamed of herself. "All right, if Gram's willing to drive you to school."

Opie skipped back toward the kitchen to complete her phone call. A moment later, she stood again in the entrance. "It's all set."

"Oh. Good."

Opie leaned against the door, hands in her pockets. She scuffed the toe of one sneaker along the floor, hanging her head as she stared at her feet, then she looked up again. "If you're sure it's okay, Mom . . ."

Marjo gazed back at her, frowning. Opie looked for all the world as if she'd done something wrong. "Honey, of course you can go see your grandparents. Any time you want."

Opie nodded, then hung her head again, studied the floor, and turned to walk through the kitchen to her room, leaving Marjo staring after her with a puzzled expression.

Ten minutes later, she came back out to the living room, carrying a folded piece of paper. "Mom?"

"Yes, Ope?"

Opie held out the paper to her. "I wrote out that recipe."

She glanced at her mother, then raised the paper again, as if, Marjo thought strangely, her conscience were bothering her.

"For Mr. Rutgers," Opie said.

CHAPTER FIVE

THURSDAY EVENING Marjo sat down to her solitary supper in an empty apartment that seemed, on a school night, disconcertingly quiet.

She washed her single dish, put in a load of laundry, checked on the dogs, and finished the last of the month's bookkeeping. Then, with most of the evening still ahead of her, she sat at the table with the evening paper, trying to enjoy the rare luxury of reading it without interruption. But the news now held little interest, and when the phone rang she reached for it eagerly, glad for a break in the silence. "Hello," she chimed into the receiver.

"Ms. Opaski? I'm a desperate man."

"Matt?" Surprise and swift warmth colored her voice.

"Yes." He sounded distracted. In the background, she could hear muffled howls and a dull, wooden rattle. He expelled a quick breath and stated, "I've got a problem."

"Oh? What?" Another howl in the background was punctuated by a series of whimpers.

She had a feeling she knew what the problem might be.

"The dog," Matt said, confirming her thoughts. "I locked him in the bathroom so I could make this call. He's not happy there."

"Not happy?" One eyebrow rose at the understatement. "It sounds like he's having a nervous breakdown."

"Yeah, well, that makes two of us. He's been doing this for five days. I can't leave him out at night or he keeps the neighbors awake. But if I leave him in the bathroom, he keeps *me* awake all night." He gave an expressive sigh. "If I don't shut him in the bathroom, he chews on the sofa legs."

Marjo felt a faint professional shudder. "I see."

"The sofa only has three legs left. It can't spare any more."

"No, I would think not."

"Look, I know it's after hours, but I was wondering if I could board him at the kennel for a couple of nights . . ."

Marjo's teaching instincts snapped into place at the request. She folded the newspaper on the table in front of her, smiled politely into the phone, and said carefully, "Of course, in emergencies, we'll always take a dog—"

She could feel relief washing over the receiver.

"—but," she qualified, "it's *not* any kind of solution to a simple training problem."

The relief was withdrawn. *"Simple?* You call this *simple?"*

"If you take him out to the car now," Marjo explained, "you're giving him the idea that howling will get him a ride in the car."

"Mmm . . . well . . . couldn't you just tell him about his genetic origins or something? God," he muttered, "do you suppose he thinks he's a wolf?"

"No," Marjo stated firmly. "He doesn't think he's a wolf. He *does* think he can get away with anything he likes in your house. He needs to be told that he can't."

A worried silence extended for a few seconds. "He doesn't seem to . . . uh . . . hear me," Matt said.

"Make him hear you. Tell him 'No!' in a firm voice."

". . . No?" Matt repeated uncertainly. His voice sounded, she reflected, about as firm as wet spaghetti. "Just tell him, 'No?'"

"If you say it with enough authority—" She broke off with an exasperated sigh. The idea of Matt having any kind of authority over his dog was clearly in the realm of wishful thinking. "Listen, maybe if you're really desperate, you could try a muzzle."

"Oh, I'm definitely desperate."

"It's only a short-term solution . . ."

"Believe me, I'll try anything. Where do I get one?"

She drummed her fingers on the folded newspaper. "I don't think you're close to any kennel-supply stores that will be open now, but I've got one here you could borrow."

"Great. I'll be—" There was a sudden pause. "Uh, Marjo?"

"Yes?"

"How do I get the dog in the car without making him think he's being rewarded for howling?"

She shook her head, chuckling. He had to be the most unpromising dog trainer she'd ever met. "Never mind. I'll bring the muzzle to you."

"Oh, hey—that's asking a lot—"

"Well, I wasn't really doing much—just sitting here alone reading the paper."

"Oh." Interested silence. "But still—" There was very little protest in his voice.

A new series of howls came over the phone line. Marjo waited with professional hope for a firmly stated

"No!" She didn't hear it. "Why don't you give me directions to your house?" she asked.

"Right," Matt said. "I'll put on a pot of coffee."

She wrote the directions on a corner of the newspaper and hung up, then went down to the supply room to find the muzzle. She caught herself humming under her breath as she jogged upstairs again to change her old jeans for gray chinos and her usual sweat shirt for—for anything else, she decided with sudden discontent.

Her wardrobe didn't offer much. She settled for a plain white cotton shirt.

In the bathroom, she got out the tube of lipstick she wore for weddings, school conferences, and holiday dinners, then hesitated before she put it on. Would he think she had dressed up—for the occasion of delivering a muzzle to his dog?

But it was only lipstick, for Pete's sake. Hardly *femme fatale* adornment. In the end, she painted her lips, then added a swipe of lipstick to each cheek and rubbed it in with her fingers. She examined her face in the mirror critically, shrugged to confirm that it didn't matter what she looked like, and turned away. Halfway to the door, she turned back and reached into the medicine cabinet for her mascara.

Matt's house was a big, square, one-story structure of the reddish landen stone that was quarried near Milwaukee and used for all kinds of locally constructed buildings and homes. The wooden trim was painted green, and an enormous weeping willow drooped over the side entry and most of the yard. Marjo parked in the driveway and shut off the car, studying the house with half-guilty curiosity. It was a home meant for a family and numerous children; comfortable, solid, far too big for one man and an unruly dog. The side porch light was on, and Marjo climbed the steps wondering whether he and his wife had planned to have a half dozen children. It was an unsettling notion.

Three seconds after her first knock, Matt answered the door, and Marjo was startled out of a last, covert examination of his backyard. She spun around, an embarrassed greeting on her lips, but at the sight of him the words stuck disconcertingly in her throat.

He was barefoot, dressed in old sweat pants and a faded sweat shirt worn into the shape of his shoulders and falling apart at the seams—obviously not the kind of attire worn to impress anyone.

She shouldn't have dressed up.

His gaze traveled down the length of her figure and back, taking in the gray chino slacks and white shirt, lingering with surprise on her made-up face. "Hi," he said finally.

"Hello." The single word sounded scratchy and ill-at-ease.

He smiled. His fascinated gaze shifted from her darkened eyelashes to her pink mouth.

She cleared her throat. "I brought the muzzle."

Matt's eyes flicked to the muzzle. "Oh, yeah." He glanced back to her face, grinned, then stepped back from the door. "Come on in."

Flash pranced toward her as she entered the back hall, wagging his tail in greeting and stepping on her foot, happily and all too clearly oblivious to any transgressions. Marjo pushed him off with practiced authority.

"Here, come on, boy." Matt pulled the dog away from her. "Sorry," he muttered. "I let him out of the bathroom after I called you."

"Mmm. Good idea." The irony was lost on Flash, who wagged his tail. She reached out to the dog, scratched his ears, and thumped his massive ribcage. He sniffed at the muzzle inquisitively, and Marjo held it out, keeping her gaze carefully averted from Matt's.

He straightened. "Hey—thanks for bringing the muzzle over. I appreciate it more than I can say."

"Oh—no problem. I was just sitting and reading the paper." She bit her lip as she realized she should have given some better excuse for her appearance. Good grief. Why was she making it so embarrassingly obvious that she'd dressed up for him?

But Matt merely shook his head and commented wryly, "Every time I try to read the paper, the damn dog finds some new way to get into trouble."

She smiled. "Well, the muzzle will keep him from chewing the sofa legs."

He nodded, then fell silent, his gaze resting on Marjo. His interest didn't seem to be on the sofa legs.

She fidgeted with the muzzle in her hands. "You just buckle this on the side, so that it fits snugly . . ."

"Okay."

Marjo searched her mind for something intelligent to say, came up blank, and finally just held out the muzzle and muttered, "Here."

"Thanks." His fingers brushed her hand as he took it. She pulled her own hand back quickly.

"You . . . uh . . . should try to catch him while he's chewing on something. Then tell him, 'No!'. If he tries again, put the muzzle on him."

Matt nodded. "Right." He jiggled the muzzle back and forth a couple of times, keeping his gaze on Marjo.

"It's important to—you've got to be firm." It was, she thought, a ridiculous thing to say when her own insides were turning to jelly. She swallowed.

Matt gestured past her to what she supposed was the kitchen. "Listen, would you like a cup of coffee?"

She hesitated, glancing around the back entryway, her gaze falling uncomfortably on the row of masculine jackets and shirts hung on wall hooks, the box of softballs in the corner, a bachelor's pile of sneakers on the floor. "I really should be going . . ."

"Come on." His mouth turned up at the corners persuasively. "You can't drive all the way over here with this thing and not at least let me give you a cup of coffee." He reached out and clasped his hand around her elbow as he turned her, with no further argument, toward the kitchen.

There was no gracious way to refuse. And no sensible reason, was there, to refuse something so innocent as a cup of coffee? She walked beside him into the kitchen, aware of the warmth of his hand. Aware, too, of the not-so-innocent flutter of her heart against her ribcage.

The dog ambled across the kitchen in front of them and sniffed with disappointment at the clean trash bin, while Matt poured coffee from the glass carafe of an automatic coffee maker into two oversized mugs. He held hers out to her. "Cream?" he asked. Before she answered, he reached into the refrigerator for the carton and handed it to her. She poured, put the carton back, and stood uneasily in the middle of the room, self-conscious in Matt's kitchen.

He gestured with his cup. "Come look at my three-legged couch."

She smiled quickly. "Do I have to sit on it?"

"Actually, it's got three and a half legs. So far, it's safe."

The three-and-half-legged couch faced a stone fireplace with a fire burning in it, casting a flickering glow to the big, dimly lit room. Paneled walls with built-in bookshelves held books, stacked magazines, and model airplanes in various stages of completion. A huge, umbrella-shaped plant with a long, twisted stem stood beside the couch, and Marjo glanced at it curiously for a moment before she realized it was a jade plant—its exotic shape due to the fact that it had been brutally pruned from the bottom up. A few chewed leaves still clung to some of the lower branches. Her gaze moved tactfully away from it. "Nice fire," she offered.

"Thanks." Matt crouched to poke at it, then leaned the poker against the stone fireplace and sat down on the couch. He gestured to his side with the mug. "Have a seat."

She sat, tentatively.

Matt stretched out his long legs and regarded her from his end of the couch. "Where's Opie tonight?"

"She's staying overnight at her grandparents' house."

"On a Thursday?" He gave her a schoolteacher's grin.

"Her grandmother is driving her to school tomorrow. Opie just wanted to see them," she added with a shrug that indicated her own perplexity. "It seemed important to her."

"Are they close? Opie and your parents?"

Marjo cast him a quick glance. "It's my ex-husband's parents she's visiting. And no, they're not especially close, but . . ." She glanced at him again, then looked away and let out a long breath. "Oh, hey," she said, a little too brightly. She reached into her pocket and pulled out a folded slip of paper. "She wrote out her recipe for you." She held out the paper to Matt and he took it, looking a little surprised.

He unfolded it to look it over, then grinned at Marjo. "I'll save this to try with Timmy."

She sketched another smile.

Matt watched her in thoughtful silence for a moment, then asked, "Is this a permission slip?"

Marjo glanced at him uncomfortably, then dropped her eyes to her coffee cup, cradling it in front of her. "I don't know what it is. I think it was more of a peace offering to me. We had a . . . sort of argument the other night." Marjo glanced at him, then peered into her coffee again, the set of her shoulders studied and a little defensive.

"After the pizza?"

She gave him another nervous smile, then shrugged. "She told me I didn't have to provide her with a father, she already has one."

"Well, that's true enough," Matt commented mildly.

Marjo's casual posture shifted abruptly. "If you could call him that." She made a cynical sound as she turned her head away from Matt; then, with sudden restlessness, jumped to her feet and paced the short distance to the fireplace. She turned, warming her backside, then asked, "Does Timmy like to cook?"

Taken aback by the quicksilver change of subject, Matt's eyebrows rose, but he said only, "Yes. He does."

"Does he bake a lot with . . . his mother?"

"No. Anne doesn't like to bake."

"Oh."

Matt studied her a moment in silence, then he said, "Anne's very ambitious. She works long hours." He smiled slightly. "She's a very good lawyer."

"Oh," she said again. "I didn't mean to pry."

"You weren't prying." He stood up and moved toward her, standing in front of her with his cup in one hand, the other resting on the mantel beside them. "You were changing the subject."

There was a long moment of silence. "I just—Opie is just—" She let out a breath.

"You use Opie as an excuse not to talk about him, don't you?" Matt said levelly.

She met his gaze with a sharp stare. "What do you mean?"

"Every time the subject of your ex-husband comes up, you start talking about Opie. It just sounds to me like Opie wasn't the only one traumatized by that marriage."

"That marriage has been over for three years!" she said a little too vehemently.

"And you don't want to talk about it, huh?"

She didn't answer for a long moment. When she glanced up at him again, his gaze was resting on her, his lips pursed thoughtfully.

She dipped her head and gave a small shrug of diffident apology, then murmured, "Look, I don't know why you'd want to talk about it anyway. . ."

The familiar, crooked grin crept up one side of his face. "Just checking out my competition, I guess."

Her cheeks flushed pink. "I—I didn't mean—I wasn't asking—"

He circled the back of her neck with one hand, his fingers warm and steady, gently kneading her tense muscles, making shivers shoot down her spine. "I didn't think you were. But some things you get without asking for them."

His fingers lightly stroked through the hair at the nape of her neck, the casual gesture intimate enough to bring all her nerve endings alive, sensuous enough to make her imagine the ways she'd like to have those fingers touch her. But Matt's words had struck a chord too close to the truth. She'd fought too hard for her independence—and her self-respect—not to have been traumatized by the battle. And she knew, all too well, how susceptible she was to the kind of touching she could imagine. Stan had been good at it, and he hadn't hesitated to use it to bend her wishes to his own. Nor had he bothered to hide his contempt for a woman who could be so easily manipulated.

She stared down into her coffee, holding herself rigid against Matt's touch.

"Tell Opie thanks for the recipe—whatever it was meant to be."

She swallowed. "Yes."

"Kids are tougher than we think, Marjo," he said softly, unexpectedly. "Opie will be fine."

The expression of serious concern in the brown eyes brought, without warning, an ache to the back of her throat, and a vulnerable tremble to her stomach. He could dissolve her resistance, she acknowledged shakily, without even trying.

Suddenly not trusting her own reactions, she stepped away from him, giving him a quavering grin over the rim of her mug, seeking to restore her crumbling defenses. "Good luck on the four-layer cake. Don't forget the green food coloring."

He laughed, letting her move away. His hand dropped back to the mantel. "I have a lifetime supply of green food coloring, Ms. Opaski," he told her. "From the green eggs."

"Oh, right. You and Opie could collaborate on a cookbook."

"I don't know about that. But maybe I could do a guide to the ten best fast-food restaurants in Milwaukee."

She gave a shaky laugh. "With video machines on the side?"

"There's something to be said for video machines."

A shiver of sexual electricity traveled down her spine, as she recalled the feel of Matt's body when they had played the video game. Again she moved away from him, on the pretext of returning to the couch. He looked for a moment as if he might follow her, but as she sat down, a movement at the corner of the fireplace caught her attention.

"Uh, Matt?"

"Yes?"

"Your dog's eating your jade plant again."

"Oh, hell!" he muttered, glancing toward the mutilated plant. "Flash! Come on, boy, leave it. Come on, leave it." He hauled the dog away from the plant with a disgusted look, then glanced back at Marjo. "He's just been fed! He can't be hungry!"

The dog peered at his master innocently, a jade leaf

hanging from the side of his mouth, and wagged his tail.

"No, he doesn't look hungry," Marjo agreed dryly.

"What am I supposed to do with him?" He gazed at the ceiling as if, she thought, an answer would appear to him by magic.

"Tell him 'No!' in a firm voice," she said.

"Oh." He glanced at her. "Yeah. Right." He made eye contact with the dog. "No."

Flash wagged his tail.

Matt glanced uncertainly back at Marjo.

"Maybe," she suggested, carefully keeping an expressionless face, "the muzzle."

"Right. The muzzle." Matt straightened, pushed his hands into his pockets and strode purposefully into the kitchen. Flash dropped down beneath what was left of the jade plant and calmly nibbled at the edge of its pot. When Matt returned with the muzzle, the dog rose to his feet, grinned trustingly up at him, and drooled a greenish stream of saliva onto the rug. Matt contemplated him morosely and glanced again at Marjo. "I don't think he'll like it."

"Probably not."

"Maybe I should . . . hold off on the muzzle."

Marjo covered her eyes with one hand and tried not to laugh at him.

"He didn't eat all that much."

She lifted her hand to examine the denuded plant, her eyebrows raised in a disbelieving arch.

"Actually"—Matt shrugged and gave an unconvincing chuckle—"there's not much more he *can* eat."

Marjo stared into her coffee, wondering if she should mention the remaining couch legs, and decided that for the moment it was a hopeless cause. Flash sank down on the hearth in front of the fire, rolled to his side, and rested his head on the flagstones with a contented sigh.

"I, uh, take it I'm being too easy on him?"

"Well..." She cast around for a tactful phrase. "Every dog owner has his own, uh, house rules, but... ah..." She trailed off. There wasn't any tactful way to say that this household didn't seem to have any rules at all.

Matt shrugged diffidently. "He's not a bad dog. He's just a little—"

"*Untrained* is the word that comes to mind," she couldn't resist commenting.

"I told him no!"

She didn't reply.

Matt let out a long sigh and shoved his hands into his pockets. "I guess I don't really have a knack for dog training," he muttered, then shot her a quick glance, vaguely hopeful of contradiction.

Her gaze moved from the self-satisfied dog to Matt's resignedly tolerant face. She should, all her professional experience told her, give him firm, direct, positive advice.

Instead, she gave in to the laughter that was brimming up from her chest. "You—" she told him, chuckling, "—are the worst dog trainer I have ever met."

He gazed back at her for a moment, his expression offended, then a broad smile spread across his face, and his eyes glinted. "Am I?" He sauntered toward her. "Well, maybe you'll just have to spend a lot more time with me." He leaned down over her, resting one hand on the back of the couch. "Would you like another cup of coffee, Ms. Opaski?"

His face, inches from hers, was lit on one side by the flickering fire, the laugh lines around his eyes softened by the warm, dim light. The back of her neck tingled where his hand had been, and her stomach still held a bubble of laughter that disarmed her resistance more surely even than the potent physical attraction that flowed between them like a magnetic current. She looked down at her coffee cup, still almost full.

A log settled in the fireplace, the small shower of sparks no more incendiary than the emotions churning in her own body. She should refuse the offer—go home—get away from this man long enough to figure out what he was doing to her.

She glanced up at him. "Maybe just a little more coffee," she said, her voice unnaturally husky.

Matt refilled her cup, then brought it back to her and sat beside her on the couch, his shoulder not quite touching hers, but his eyes seductive as they rested on her hands, the side of her face, her eyelashes.

She stared into her coffee, not sure why she'd accepted it, telling herself it was just casually offered, casually accepted hospitality. But it was impossible to ignore her own increased heartbeat or the way Matt was looking at her. Or the fact that her body was radiating enough warmth to rival the fireplace.

"I . . . should probably be going," she said indistinctly.

Matt leaned forward to set his own mug on the floor, then sat back and stretched his arm along the back of the couch behind her.

"I—uh—" She smiled inanely. "Early to bed, early to rise, as they say—"

He smiled at her, the smile slow, sexy, and amused. "—gets the worm?"

"I wasn't going to say anything about worms," she muttered.

"No?" His hand drifted over the curve of her shoulder. A shiver of sensuality ran down the back of her neck.

"Good," he said softly. "I didn't want to talk about worms anyway." He moved imperceptibly closer to her. His fingers trailed up along the side of her neck to her earlobe.

"Matt . . . I . . . I don't know . . ."

Barely touching her, he traced the curve of her ear. "You know what they say, Ms. Opaski."

"What?"

He smiled slowly. "If you can't take the fleas, get out of the kennel." He reached around her for her cup of coffee, then leaned to put it on the floor beside his own.

She watched him, wide-eyed, mesmerized, making no move whatever to get out of the kennel.

His hand slid down across her shoulder, and he turned her slightly toward him. "And you know what they say," he murmured, his face inches from hers, "about looking a gift horse . . . in the mouth."

Her eyes involuntarily dropped to his mouth, just before he came too close for her to see it and his lips touched hers, soft, warm, gently persuasive—and entirely unresisted. The bubble of laughter in her chest dissolved like warm taffy into a sweet, rich melting of her defenses as his hands began to move on her back, slowly, exploratively, with unhurried sensuality. Gently, he pulled her closer to him, while his head tipped sideways and his mouth moved slightly, gently, over hers. He guided her arms around his neck, hesitating a moment, as if to see if she would keep them there. For Marjo, there seemed to be no choice. Her palms flattened against his shoulders, seeking contact and warmth, moving against his shirt as if of their own will.

Matt wrapped his arms around her again, drawing her still closer. She felt the flick of his tongue, entreating, tempting, seductive. Something that had been closed and locked in an inner corner of her mind opened to aching warmth in her body. Her lips parted. She met his seeking tongue with her own, and felt an electrifying, intimate thrill.

His fingers threaded up through her hair until his palms were resting against the back of her head. He caressed the hollows beneath her ears as he tipped her head against the back of the couch and moved his mouth over hers, seeking, commanding, holding her captive for a kiss where the capture had become complete surrender.

Her heart hammered against her chest, and her stomach trembled with stirring desire as she lost herself in the kiss—the warm, wet caress of his tongue around the inner edge of her lips . . . the exciting texture of his mouth against hers . . . the tantalizing brush of his thumbs against the skin of her neck.

He shifted on the couch to bring their bodies closer together, chest to chest, and she felt his heartbeats, in counterrhythm to hers, as his hips started another rhythm against the side of her thigh. Without thought, she moved to accommodate him, sliding down on the couch and turning her hips more squarely to his, instinctively seeking the hard ridge of his body that gave proof to his desire.

With sudden urgency, he broke off the kiss. His lips traced the line of her jaw, the side of her neck, the hollow above her collarbone.

She made an almost inaudible sound in the back of her throat as she realized, suddenly, what she was inviting, and turned her head away from him as she straightened on the couch, drawing in a deep, shaky breath. Matt lifted his head from her neck, drew in his own shuddering breath, and leaned his forehead against her chin. Slowly, as if with great concentration, he uncurled his fingers from her hair and slid his hands out along her shoulders.

"I didn't—" The words came out as a hoarse croak, and he took another breath before he repeated them. "I didn't mean to take things this fast," he told her. His breath sent warm tremors against her throat.

She let out a huff of tight, taken-by-surprise laughter. "No, neither did I." The words were a high-pitched, unnatural squeak. She swallowed convulsively, embarrassed at her own responses, wondering if Matt Rutgers would think she was . . . forward. Her gaze fell on his hair, brown, thick, slightly curly, and the urge to touch it, to run her fingers through it, was just barely resistible.

He pulled away from her and sat up, then pulled her up against him, tucking her head into the hollow of his shoulder and resting his hands at her waist. His breath fanned the hair at the top of her forehead, its rhythm as fast-paced as her own pulse, which seemed unwilling to slow down despite the voice of common sense that told her she was, indeed, taking things too fast.

"What did you put in that coffee?" she managed with a shaky laugh.

A chuckle rumbled in his chest beneath her ear. "A secret formula. Passed down from a long line of lousy dog trainers, one to the other."

She chuckled with him for a moment. "Oh, I see." She pulled away and sat up straight on the couch, reaching for her cup as if to keep her hands from temptation.

Matt let his arms fall away from her shoulders, but his gaze never left her face. "I could make another pot," he teased, giving her his crooked grin and the warmest of glints in his eyes.

For a moment, the urge to accept his invitation was so strong that it sent a twinge of panic up from her stomach. She laughed again, her voice husky. "I think I've had enough of your coffee for tonight."

His grin faded slowly away as he studied her face. "Marjo—"

She cut him off before he could say something that would erase her fragile resistance. "I really should be going." Her glance flicked off his face, then skittered back again like a nervous butterfly.

Matt returned her gaze, his own expression serious, then he nodded once and smiled slightly. "Okay, then."

He didn't object when she stood up, but simply got

up himself, shoving his hands into his pockets, making no move to touch her again.

"Well . . ." She leaned down to give Flash a pat, then turned toward the kitchen, her cup still in hand. Matt followed her, silent, into the kitchen, then caught her elbow to turn her around. "You planning to walk off with my cup, Ms. Opaski?"

"Oh—no—I—"

He took it from her numb fingers and set it on the counter, then grinned at her: warm . . . sexy . . . tempting.

She shoved her own hands into her pockets. "Well . . . good night."

He nodded. The grin slipped, again, into a serious expression. "Good night," he repeated gruffly, then, with no hint of a smile, "You'd better get going, Ms. Opaski, if you really expect to go."

She nodded once, swallowed, then turned and let herself out through the back hall, unsure of whether she was fleeing from temptation or merely obeying orders that were not, in the least, appealing.

CHAPTER SIX

IT RAINED THE following day. As the morning drizzle turned into an afternoon downpour, Marjo counted off the hours until Matt's five o'clock lesson with growing impatience, chiding herself for acting like a lovestruck teenager every time she looked at the clock, but nonetheless checking it with regularity.

Opie had been busy on some project of her own since she'd gotten home from school, but she appeared, unannounced, to help her mother straighten the indoor training room just before the five o'clock lesson. Marjo accepted her help with no comment. She hadn't yet managed to decipher her own motives, and she was no closer to understanding them when Matt, Tim, and the dog entered the training room, leaving three sets of muddy footprints in their wake.

Matt looked up at her, ignoring the footprints, and smiled. "Ms. Opaski," he said.

That smile was everything a lovestruck teenager could have wished for. She took a deep breath, found her voice, and muttered, "Hi."

Tim cleared his throat. "Uh, Dad?"

"Hmm?" Matt glanced from Marjo to his son.

"Flash is chewing on his leash."

"Oh—hey—stop that. Flash! Cut it out."

The dog wagged his tail in languid acknowledgment while he continued chewing, and Marjo waited for the sharp reprimand that never, of course, came.

"Dad?"

"Hmm?"

"Should I . . . uh . . . take over, sort of?"

Matt glanced from the dog to his son to Marjo, then thrust the end of the leash toward Tim. "Sure. You take over."

Tim gave Opie a knowing look, but the girl merely shrugged with exaggerated nonchalance, then turned her interest to the shelves of supplies, her casual stance telegraphing the message that she was too sophisticated to show an interest.

With Tim training the dog, the lesson proceeded smoothly. The boy needed little guidance from Marjo, and her attention was drawn to Matt like the tide to the moon. She was overwhelmingly aware of him, standing just beside her, hands clasped behind him as he whistled a snatch of tune from a popular rock ballad. Unerringly, her mind put the words to it; inevitably, they were appropriate: *When I'm near you I can't think of anything else . . .*

She brought her gaze sharply back to the dog, but her attention stayed with Matt. And despite everything— her concern with Opie, her effort to concentrate on the lesson, and the awkwardness of flirting with a man who'd brought his own ten-year-old chaperon—her lips curved in an impossible-to-resist smile. He was incorrigible. Not to mention persistent and imaginative. Not to mention incredibly . . . sexy.

By the end of the hour, she was struggling to keep her own imagination in line. Tim didn't require any instructions beyond "Keep up the good work, Tim," and a sincere smile that was matched by his father's beaming approval as he gave his son a one-armed hug, then grinned at Marjo with easy enjoyment of Timmy's accomplishment. Marjo couldn't help smiling back.

The crooked grin lingered on her face for a moment, then Matt dropped his arm, pushed his hands slowly into his pockets, and crossed the room to stand in front of her.

There was an interval of curious silence from Tim, Opie, and the dog as Matt reached into his shirt pocket and pulled out a small stack of tickets. He glanced over his shoulder to catch the interested stares of his audience, then looked back at Marjo and mentioned, ever-so-casually, "I have tickets to the ball game tomorrow. I thought we might all want to go to it."

"Oh, yeah, Dad—that's a great idea," Tim piped up enthusiastically.

Opie, Marjo, and Flash were conspicuously silent. Marjo shot her daughter an assessing glance, wondering what Opie's response would be, but the girl's face was blank and uninformative. Marjo glanced back at Matt.

He smiled slowly into her eyes and waited.

"You thought . . . we'd all like to go to it?" she stalled.

"Well—" He shrugged, teasing her, "I know you don't really like baseball . . ."

Tim's jaw dropped open and he turned an expression of stunned incredulity on Opie. "Your mother doesn't like baseball?"

Matt's smile widened. "Grown men sliding around in the dirt. Crowds of people shouting and jumping up and down. Hot dogs and beer. All-American fun . . ."

"My mother likes baseball!" Opie told Tim indignantly.

"Matt . . . I . . ."

He leaned imperceptibly closer to her. His gaze dropped for just a fraction of a second to her lips, and she felt heat rise in her cheeks, half in memory of the kiss they had shared the night before, half in outrage at his machinations.

"Matt . . . I don't—"

"—like baseball," he finished for her, the glint in his eye becoming more impudent by the second. "But maybe you ought to think about the House Un-American Activities Committee, Ms. Opaski."

"She *said* she doesn't like it," Tim told Opie.

"She does so like it!"

"Matt," she repeated in exasperation, "this is not the time to—"

His eyes drifted down to her shoulder, then back up along the side of her neck to the edge of her jaw. He studied the heightened color along her cheekbones, then finally met her flustered gaze. "To what?" he asked, all innocence.

"Mom! Tell Tim you like baseball!" Opie demanded.

Marjo glanced at her daughter, looked back at Matt's carefully guileless expression, then shook her head and gave in to the chuckle that finished off the last of her meager argument. He was impossible! "All right! All right! I like baseball. I like watching grown men sliding around in the dirt. I admit it!"

Matt's grin turned self-satisfied. "Good. We'll pick you up at four. Okay?"

"Okay."

Matt smiled over his shoulder at Opie. "You like hot dogs, Opie?"

The girl shrugged indifferently, then relented enough to say, "Yeah, I like hot dogs."

He turned back to Marjo. His lips drifted down into an expression she recognized. It set off butterflies in her stomach. He lingered there a long moment, his hands behind his back, while Marjo's imagination supplied the ungiven kiss in vivid detail, then, without having touched her, he nodded, slid the tickets back into his pocket, and said softly, "See you tomorrow."

He turned back to Tim, put a hand on his shoulder, then followed his son and the dog out, whistling "Take Me Out to the Ball Game" as he went.

Matt arrived at four on the dot, and Marjo and Opie were ready and waiting in the parking lot, Marjo dressed to make a point, in a red and white Penn State jersey and blue pants. He grinned as he got out of the car, looking her over with approval.

"Very—patriotic, Ms. Opaski," he commented. "Not at all un-American."

Her answering grin was smugly complacent. "I told you, I like baseball."

He opened the car door for her, whistling "The Star-Spangled Banner" and letting his eyes run down over the backside of her blue chinos as she climbed in.

Saturday afternoon traffic was light, and they arrived in plenty of time for the five o'clock game, but even so, the stadium was crowded, rows of cars already filling in the parking lot as Matt turned down an aisle and found a space halfway to the stadium.

Street vendors around the stadium were selling everything from cheese curds to Brewers pennants to brockwurst, the ethnic specialties as popular as hot dogs with the diverse, quintessentially American population of Milwaukee. Connoisseurs of Polish, Italian, and German cuisine were giving the stands a brisk trade as Matt and Marjo followed the crowds, walking behind Tim and Opie toward the stadium entrance. Matt swung an arm around Marjo's shoulders, pulling her in close beside him and matching his step to hers.

She glanced at him through thick lashes, then looked away, making no comment, but he could tell from the quick tightening of her shoulders that the casual contact affected her as much as it did him; he wanted much more than casual contact.

Marjo's half-guilty gaze sought out her daughter, as

if to check Opie's reaction to her mother's walking hip-
to-hip with a man, but Opie was paying no attention,
strolling beside Tim, apparently involved in a desultory
discussion. She looked a little more subdued than was
her usual style, but not unhappy. Matt glanced back at
Marjo.

"Opie didn't mind coming to the game, did she?"

Marjo shook her head. "No, she didn't seem to."

"Good. I didn't want her to feel roped into it."

She gave him a quick, impish grin that made the
freckles on her nose stand out. "I thought I was the one
being roped into it."

He acknowledged his stratagem with a grin. "Ve haf
our vays, Mzzz Opassski." He slowed their steps as he
ran his hand down her arm in a slow caress. His gaze
drifted down over her jersey and chinos, then rested a
moment on her lightly made-up face. He said softly,
"You look very pretty today."

He watched the color heighten in her face in the reaction he'd been looking for. It set up a response in him
that needed further exploration. And privacy.

He glanced once at the disappearing backs of their
children, then pulled Marjo to a stop. "Tim will wait for
us at the entrance."

Two couples brushed by them, laughing and talking,
on their way to the game. Marjo peered around their
heads, looking after the kids, and Matt turned her back
toward him, his hands on her shoulders. "They'll wait
for us," he repeated.

"Oh, I know. It's just—"

"You worry about her," he stated. His hands slid
down to her shoulders. "About how she feels about us."

"I—yes."

"Want me to talk to her?"

"I don't think she'd talk to you, Matt. She's always
talked just to me, since—the divorce."

He studied her a moment. "Must be hard, doing it all yourself."

She shrugged against the weight of his hands and gave him an automatic smile. "Nothing I can't handle."

He didn't smile back. He touched the bridge of her nose with an index finger, then traced the path of freckles across her cheekbone. "And no one should have the nerve to offer you any help, right?"

She drew in a breath that she didn't let out, and her eyelids fluttered down. "I don't mean to sound like that. I mean—" She swallowed. "I mean—thanks for—for taking an interest in Opie."

"She's not hard to take an interest in. She's a lot like you, you know." His fingers threaded into her hair. "Independent, self-reliant, tough on the outside, soft on the inside . . ." He leaned down to close the distance between them. The kiss was quick, intense, and not nearly enough to satisfy him, but Matt straightened, glanced toward the place where Tim and Opie had last been seen, then grinned into Marjo's flushed face. "Come on. There's a ball game going on here." He gave her shoulders a final squeeze as he added, "Everything will work out. You'll see."

Tim was waiting impatiently when they caught up. "Come on, Dad. Let's go."

Marjo glanced around them at the crowd, as if just noticing it, and commented, "I thought we were early enough to be ahead of everyone."

"Not for this game," Matt said. "It's the first home game in three weeks, and the last time we played the Red Sox we lost by one run in the eleventh."

"Yeah," Tim added. "With two men on." He turned impatiently toward the gate, adding something that sounded like, "And Old-man-ski's pitching."

"Who?" Opie queried as she followed him.

Inside the entrance gate, Tim glanced toward his father.

"We're gonna win this one, Dad."

"You're sure about that?"

"I bet you the dishes tomorrow morning."

Matt grinned. "You're on."

Marjo smiled at both of them when Matt looked up at her, but Opie followed the exchange with frowning concentration, obviously disturbed by some inner thoughts of her own, then trailed after Tim, still frowning, as he headed purposefully toward the section of the stands behind third base.

Their seats were in two rows. Opie and Tim elected to sit in front of their parents, and they'd climbed in over several pairs of feet before Tim realized he was thirsty. Matt shook his head, sighed with resigned good nature, and climbed back out again in search of soda and popcorn.

Opie gazed after him for a moment, letting out a long sigh, then turned a long face back toward Tim. He returned the perusal curiously. Opie dropped her eyes to her shoes and bent, greatly absorbed with retying one sneaker. Then she asked casually, "Does your father take you to ball games a lot?"

"Yeah, pretty much." There was a silent pause. "Does yours?"

Opie gave him a sharp glance, and Marjo leaned forward to intercede, but the girl seemed able to handle the question herself. She shrugged indifferently. "No, not very much."

"Oh."

"He doesn't live near here, so he can't take me to ball games and stuff."

"Oh, yeah." Tim nodded.

Opie gave him another scowl, then went on a little belligerently, "You can't always pick where you're gonna live, you know."

Marjo glanced from the back of Opie's stiff spine to

Tim's puzzled expression, feeling a twinge of anxiety form in the pit of her stomach.

"No," he said. "I guess not."

"Well, you can't!"

"I didn't say you could!"

"Opie's been to a couple of games with her grandparents," Marjo put in. She leaned forward and put a hand on her daughter's shoulder. "Haven't you, Ope?"

Opie glanced at her, then nodded. "Well, one, anyway."

"And—and fathers aren't the only ones who can take kids places. Opie and I go to a lot of other things—the science museum, obedience trials—"

"That's not the same thing, Mom," Opie muttered to her shoes, but Tim glanced from Marjo to Opie with interest.

"You go to obedience trials? What's it like?"

"Oh . . ." Opie shrugged again, but brightened a little as she started on her favorite topic. "It's pretty neat. Especially, you know, when you've got your own dog in it, like Flash or someone."

Marjo leaned back, temporarily grateful for Tim's interest in a subject where Opie could shine. But why did the subject of Opie's father have to come up today? She let out a breath and involuntarily glanced toward the end of the row where Matt had gone to find sodas and popcorn.

Matt returned, stumbling over the annoyed feet again just as the opening pitch was thrown out, connected with a solid crack against the batter's swing, and was caught handily by the infielder closest to them. Tim leaped to his feet, groaning with disappointment, along with most of the row of people beside them. A burly fan in a red-checked shirt sitting in front of Tim raised one fist and shouted, "What kind of a pitch was that, ya lousy bum!"

Matt had all he could do to save the tray of drinks

from disaster. Marjo gave him a smile as he settled in safely beside her, but she moved over enough to put a small distance between them, as she glanced at the back of Opie's blonde head, then looked down at her lap. Opie hadn't mentioned her father since the night of their argument, but she'd been, at times, moody and evasive, and Marjo couldn't quite dispel the unease that dampened her enjoyment of the day, and cast a pall of self-doubt over her feelings for the man sitting next to her.

Everything would work out, he'd told her. But she'd been told that before. Usually with a rider implying that her own lack of faith was the reason things had failed to work out in the past.

Her mouth quirked at one corner in cynical irony. For years she'd had inexhaustible supplies of faith, and it hadn't moved Stan Wozniak one mustard seed's worth. She'd learned to rely on common sense and hard work —her own.

She shot a quick glance at Matt, then forced her eyes away from the dark hair, the clean profile, the ready, endearing grin, and stared down at the soda she clutched in her hands, her thoughts troubled.

By the bottom of the third inning the score was 2 to 0, Sox, and Tim's optimism was fading. "Doesn't look too good for me, huh, Dad?" he commented to his father.

Matt grinned back. "Mmm. Not much of a loss, though, now that I think of it. It was your turn to do the dishes on Sunday anyway, wasn't it?"

"Oh, yeah. I guess it was."

Opie's glance skittered from Matt to Tim and back as they talked. When Tim turned to face the game again, she gave him a smug look. "You ought to get a dishwasher. My mom has one."

"Yeah. My mom has one, too."

Opie's face fell.

"Dad was gonna get one," Tim continued, "but when

we figured out the budget, we decided to buy models instead."

"Models of a dishwasher?"

Tim gave her a look. "Model planes. That's one of our hobbies. We build model planes and fly them."

Opie was silent, her mouth set in a stubborn line. Matt leaned down between the two children and put in, "Opie bakes cakes, Tim. She gave us the recipe for that great one she invented—the four-layer one."

"You invented a cake?" Tim asked.

Opie nodded warily.

"My mom invents cakes sometimes," Tim put in thoughtlessly, "and Dad and I—"

"Hot dog, Opie?" Matt interjected. "Tim, you want a hot dog?"

"Oh, yeah. Great," Tim agreed.

Subdued, Opie said, "Okay," and Matt nodded and smiled at her, then glanced out along the row of feet between him and the hot dogs. He exchanged a look with Marjo, one corner of his mouth quirked up in martyred resignation.

She glanced away from that conspiratorial, parents-have-to-stick-together look, uneasy with the implication that she and Matt were an established team. "I'll go." She set her soda down and stood up.

"No, no—I'll go."

But she was already murmuring apologies as she made her way down to the end of the row.

Munching popcorn and ignoring Opie's prickly silence, Tim was telling her about his weekend schedule. "I get out early on Fridays," he explained between mouthfuls. "My mom drives me to Dad's."

"Oh, that must be great," Opie commented sarcastically.

Tim turned toward her, a handful of popcorn halted halfway to his mouth. "What do you mean?"

"Oh, *you* know"—Opie shrugged and reached for her own popcorn—"having the two of them together."

"What's wrong with having the two of them together?"

"Well, *you* know!"

"No. What?"

Matt's gaze moved from Tim to Opie. He frowned, waiting for Opie's answer.

She gestured in exasperation. "Well—they probably don't want to talk about each other, you know? And you have to be so careful not to talk about the other one, and not bring up certain subjects and stuff, and—I don't know! If you don't understand what I mean, I'm not going to explain it."

Tim stared at her, slow-dawning awareness of Opie's point of view occurring to him. "My parents don't—uh —mind talking to each other. I mean, maybe it's just, well, your mom's problem."

Matt groaned silently at Tim's tactlessness. Opie glared at Tim belligerently. "What do you know about it?" she spouted.

Matt leaned forward in his seat. "Opie, Tim's mother and I have been—"

The girl spun around toward him, surprised at his voice. The soda in her hand caught Tim's elbow and the drink toppled into the boy's lap, splashing onto his shirt and spilling down his pants.

"Hey! For Pete's sake—" Tim jumped up, brushing ice cubes off his lap, dripping from chest to knees. "Geez!" he accused Opie.

"Well, you were right in the way!"

"I was in the way? You're the one that spilled the drink, for Pete's sake!"

Opie leaped to her feet beside him. "Oh, you think you're so great! Just because your father takes you to ball games and makes stupid models and stuff!"

Heads were turning around them. The man in the

red-checked shirt twisted in his seat to see what was going on. At the end of the aisle, past half a row of annoyed spectators, Matt caught sight of Marjo, hot-dog tray in hand, her stricken gaze fixed on her daughter. He turned back to the two kids, with the sinking feeling of having definitely failed to avert a crisis.

"You don't have to get so mad about it," Tim spouted back at Opie. "He's taking you, too!"

"Tim—" Matt put in. "Opie—"

"I don't know what she's so mad about!" Tim protested in outraged innocence. *"She's* the one that spilled the drink!"

"I don't need to have somebody else's father take me to ball games!" Opie glared from Tim to Matt, her eyes bright with threatened tears. "I have a father!"

Matt pulled a handkerchief from his back pocket and handed it to Tim, who mopped at his wet shirt, tightening his mouth in anger, while Matt watched Opie in silence for a moment, then said quietly, "Of course you have a father, Opie."

Opie blinked rapidly and clutched her popcorn box against her stomach.

"And it's understandable that you'd want to spend more time with him, Ope, but fathers can't always choose their schedules. You were right about that."

"Yeah," Opie answered, her voice defensive. "They can't."

"Or where they have to live."

"That's right." She sniffed and nodded again.

Matt offered her a slight smile. "We should sit down," he suggested.

Opie looked around self-consciously at the people sitting near them. The red-shirted man in front of Tim returned her glance with good-natured curiosity. "Yeah," he muttered at the girl. "You're here now, aren't ya? Why don't ya watch the game?" He turned back to the ball field. "C'mon ya bums, let's see some action!"

Opie sat down, still clutching her popcorn. "Sorry I spilled the soda," she muttered to Tim after a moment.

"That's all right."

The argument was over when Marjo got back to her place. She looked from the back of her daughter's head to Matt, her face troubled. He gave her a quick smile and a silent "Okay" sign with thumb and forefinger, but her worried gaze dropped to her lap once again, and she refused to acknowledge the smile.

"Hot dog, Ope?" Matt offered. "Tim?"

"Okay."

"Sure."

He handed out hot dogs, then gave the extra napkins to Tim. "We can get another soda, Ope, when they come around with them."

"Okay," she said again. She sat, holding her hot dog, facing toward the game.

Matt leaned toward her casually as he took a paper cup full of beer from Marjo's tray. "What does your father do, Opie?"

The girl turned toward him, shot a quick glance at her mother, then told Matt, "He's a D.J. In Rapid City, South Dakota."

"Oh, yeah?" Tim asked. "That's neat. What radio station?"

"WKLD."

"What kind of show does he do?" Matt asked her.

"Talk shows. You know, where people call in."

"Neat," Tim repeated.

"He's been at this same station for a year and a half," Opie added after a moment, as if testing out the effect of her words. She glanced sideways at her mother, her look furtive and half-guilty, then went on, "He just got a promotion. And he's thinking about trying to get a job closer to here."

"Hey, that'd be great," Tim offered. "Then you could listen to him."

"Yeah. Maybe." Opie bit into her hot dog and munched with satisfaction.

The red-shirted fan raised his hands to his mouth and bellowed toward the players, "Home run! Home run! C'mon, home run!" He kept up the litany until he'd started a chorus of his neighbors around him. Tim put down his soda to shout, "Home run!" along with the others. Opie gave him a startled look, then joined in.

Matt glanced at Marjo. She was frowning at her daughter, her face marked with bewilderment.

"Your ex-husband is a D.J.?" Matt asked.

"I didn't know what he was doing for a living." She glanced at her daughter, perturbed. "Opie must have found out from her grandparents."

"Oh." He sipped his beer, then gave her a wry smile. "Well, you never know what you're going to learn at a ball game."

She didn't smile back.

"Hey." He put a hand on her shoulder, speaking softly. "Come on. It's not that serious."

Marjo glanced down at her beer, silent.

Matt studied her for a moment. "I think she just needs to know she has a father, Marjo."

"Maybe." She sipped her beer, then lowered the cup with a nervous, indecisive gesture and blurted out, "I didn't know she ever talked about him!"

"Hell, every kid wants two parents. And even an absent one is better than none at all."

"Oh, he's absent, all right," Marjo commented bitterly. When Matt gave no reply, she glanced up at him, then dropped her gaze, embarrassed at the animosity of her tone.

"Opie's proud of him, Marjo."

Marjo bit her lip to stop its sudden trembling as she

looked up once again at Matt. "I just don't want her hurt."

"I know." He slid his arm around her shoulders and pulled her a little closer to him. She resisted, stiffening her spine against Matt's pressure, but he pulled her in close to his side anyway.

"I can't stand the thought of Opie being hurt," she said in a small, choked voice.

"I know," he said again. He kept his arm around her, close and protecting.

She let her eyes slide shut, allowed herself to lean, tentatively, against Matt's strong shoulder, and took a long, unsteady breath. Matt's arm was heavy across her back, his fingers warm where they curled around her upper arm. He smelled faintly of citrus. She'd never noticed his after shave. He must have put it on, she realized with a small jolt of perception, for her. He smelled good. And he felt good—very good. Too good. Confusion warred with the physical yearnings she felt for him, her worry about her daughter at odds with the wish to trust to instinct—trust that things would, indeed, work out. She swallowed a lump of tears that tightened her throat.

Matt glanced down at her, then gave her shoulder a little shake, as if she were Tim. "You can't keep her in a glass case, Marjo," he said softly. "We all risk getting hurt. You can't live without risk."

She was silent a moment. "I don't think," she murmured against Matt's shoulder, "I'm much of a gambler."

"You don't?" he challenged. "You don't think it was a gamble to start your own kennel?"

"I—I don't—"

"Or to buy the building?"

"It was—"

"Or to try to make it on your own in the first place?"

She fell silent in the face of that unshakable conviction, unable to deny his questions but unwilling to give up the anxious worry that churned in her stomach.

His arm tightened around her. "Come on," he said again. "We're at a ball game. Opie looks like she's having a great time. She'll be okay."

The chorus of "Home run! Home run!" had swelled to a crescendo, Opie and Tim adding their parts with gusto. The burly fan who had started the shouting was now pounding his feet in time to the words. Marjo glanced around her, then looked back at Matt, her mouth curved in a wan smile that didn't reach her eyes. "Seems like everyone else is, too."

"That's what you're supposed to do at a ball game. If you can't be one of the grown men sliding around in the dirt, you can at least bellow at them from the stands."

Her smile tilted her lips once more, and again Matt's free hand came up to stroke the side of her face, then slid under the hair at the back of her neck as he turned her toward him.

"Dad?"

They moved abruptly apart at the sound of Tim's voice.

"What?" Matt asked him.

"The—uh—man with the soda is coming down the rows over there."

"Um." Matt's eyes followed Tim's gesture, then he pulled change from his back pocket and handed it to his son. "You go get it this time."

"Sure. Thanks." Tim headed toward the soda while Opie turned back toward her mother and Matt with a wide grin.

"We almost got 'em, huh?"

"Oh—uh—yeah." Matt scanned the ball field, nodding absently.

"I missed that play," he muttered at Marjo when Opie had turned back. "I don't suppose you saw it?"

She shook her head, smiling a little again.

"Oh, that's right." He nodded sagely, but there was a hint of mischief in his eyes. "You don't like baseball."

"I do so like baseball. Especially when I don't have to play."

"Ahh, Ms. Opaski . . ." He shook his head. "You've just never had the pleasure, I have to assume, of sliding around in the dirt."

"I suppose we can't all get to slide around in the dirt."

"Play your cards right, Ms. Opaski, and I'll give you your chance."

"No, thanks," she declined playfully. "I'd just get grass stains on my shirt, and I do my own laundry."

"You don't have enough vices, Ms. Opaski."

Her lips tilted up fractionally at the corners. "I can't afford vices."

"You could start with the free ones."

"Free vices?"

"Yeah. I could put a list of them at the end of my book about fast-food places." He tipped his head to one side and quirked his mouth, considering. "Or I could write it up as an article for *Wisconsin Life.* 'Vice on a Shoestring.' 'The Primrose Path on Five Dollars a Day.'" He narrowed his eyes at her. "'Vice in Visconsin.'"

"In Visconsin?"

He made a sound of mock disgust. "That's the trouble with Wisconsin women. They have no imagination."

"No hope for us Visconsin Vomen, I guess."

"Oh, I don't know." He peered down at her, the beginnings of a grin playing around his mouth. "Maybe we could work on it."

She fell silent for a moment, her head still resting against his shoulder. "What did you have in mind?"

He raised an eyebrow at her, but his eyes glinted mischievously. "Something . . . risky."

"Oh, no—no race-car driving," she stipulated, shaking her head emphatically. "I look terrible in crash helmets."

"I thought we were quite a team as race-car drivers."

"We crashed a lot."

"Mmm." He grinned at her, the kind of slow smile that made her pulse beat faster.

Looking into those bedroom eyes was risky enough, she decided, for a whole book about vice. Her imagination seemed to be working just fine. "So—what did you have in mind?" she repeated.

"Let's go stargazing. On the lake."

"Stargazing?" Her voice rose in surprise. "On the lake?"

"I have an eighteen-foot outboard."

"Oh."

"Next Saturday night. What do you say?"

"I—I don't know." She bit her lip, doubt creeping back into her voice. "Something might come up with the dogs—"

He circled her shoulders again with his arm and glanced down at her, his smile gone. "What do you say, Marjo?"

His face, almost in profile, was close enough that she could smell citrus, could count the fine laugh lines at his eyes and the brackets around his mouth that showed how easily he smiled, could imagine the things that smile did to her.

But he wasn't smiling. His mouth was set in a resolute line, the eyes serious, asking for an honest reckoning of her feelings. And he was sitting close enough to make her stomach tremble; close enough to make common sense as remote as the Antarctic. *A new man in her life.* The thought engraved itself on her mind as if it had belonged there for weeks.

She said yes.

CHAPTER SEVEN

MARJO HAD DROPPED Opie at her grandparents' house, and was ready an hour before Matt arrived the following Saturday. She had paced over to the window a dozen times before she gave up any pretense of doing anything and stood staring out at the driveway, waiting for him. The week's two lessons with Flash had been attended by both Timmy and Opie, and the idea of seeing Matt with his eighteen-foot boat and without chaperons was—she smiled to herself—romantic. She had visions of something trim and white, with sails.

Matt's familiar station wagon pulled into her parking lot five minutes early. He was towing behind him an eighteen-foot boat that could only be described as ancient.

Marjo stood where she was at the window, looking at the boat in fascinated dismay. The white paint was peeling from the small deck at the bow, the Mercury outboard had obviously seen better days, and the whole rig sat on the trailer with a decided list. She was still staring at the boat, her expression disbelieving, when Matt crossed the parking lot and rang her bell.

"Here she is," Matt commented when Marjo came

down to meet him. He took her elbow to lead her around to the parking lot where the boat and his station wagon were waiting. Marjo examined the boat in silence.

Apparently unaware of her skepticism, Matt gave the sky a leisurely appraisal, glancing off to the west, where the sun was just touching the rim of low hills. "Looks like a good night for stargazing."

There was a pause while Marjo glanced back again to the boat. "On the lake?" she asked finally.

"Mmm. It's a calm evening. Not much wind." He smiled down at her. "We can get a ways out from shore so the lights of the city won't dim the view."

Marjo made an inarticulate sound that managed to convey very articulate doubts. "How far out are you planning to get?"

"Oh . . ." He shrugged. "A quarter of a mile."

"We're going a quarter of a mile away from shore in *that?*"

"That's a she. Boats are always she."

"Yes, well . . ." Marjo gave him a weak smile and searched for a tactful remark. "She just—doesn't look very seaworthy."

"She's perfectly seaworthy." He looked offended; then, glancing at the boat, doubtfully evasive. "She needs a little paint, maybe . . . I meant to paint her over the winter, but I never quite got to it." He shrugged again, casually, and mentioned, "I bought a new line for towing her, though."

"Oh." Marjo squinted at the new rope tied to the bow of the boat and nodded without enthusiasm.

"We did agree to do something risky."

She opened her mouth to object, but there were glints in his eyes that warned her he was teasing her. And enjoying it. She bit her lip, determined not to give him the satisfaction of showing her nervousness, then asked, unable to stop herself, "Doesn't it lean a little to the right?"

"Starboard. On a boat it's always starboard."

"Matt." She drew herself up to her full height and looked him in the eye, tipping her chin up to do it. *"Does it float?"*

His grin faded into a sober expression, and he assured her solemnly, "Yes, she floats. I had her in the water last fall."

"Thank you," she told him.

He gave her a sidelong glance, pensively sucking in his cheeks. "You *can* swim, can't you?"

As if in echo of her own outrage, there was a howl from the back of the station wagon.

Marjo recognized the voice.

Matt gave her a smile that, this time, looked apologetic, and explained, "I tried to leave him at home, but he . . . ah . . . protested." He swung his arm around her shoulders and pulled her in close beside him. "You don't mind, do you?" he asked.

Her arm brushed against the hard wall of his well-muscled torso, and her hip touched his as they matched steps to the car. He was wearing the same citrus-scented after shave he'd had on at the ball game, and the last rays of sunlight touched his brown hair with gold glints that matched the glints in those dark eyes.

He could have, she decided, brought a whole menagerie with him; it wouldn't have affected in the least what he did to her senses when he was near her. *A new man in her life*. She glanced up into the brown eyes and smiled. "No, I guess not. As long as he can swim."

There was a boat launch area, Matt told her, at the South Shore Marina and Yacht Club. They could put the boat in at the launch ramp and head out from there.

Marjo gave him a dubious smile. "We'll fit right in with the other yachts."

"Hey." He grinned. "A boat's a boat, right?"

"Oh, right." And a grin, she thought with her heart thudding erratically in response to it, was a grin. And a kiss was a kiss... And here she was, headed out into deep water with a man who made her think of song lyrics at odd moments.

And with a dog. One shouldn't, she reflected, forget the dog.

Matt made the mistake of forgetting the dog when they stopped at the boat launching ramp to negotiate the tricky maneuver of backing the trailer into the water.

Flash headed straight for the lake, ears flapping, and plunged in with joy, splashing a couple of ice-cream-eating teenagers perched on a retaining wall near the ramp and gleefully ignoring his master's shouts.

By the time Matt had retrieved him, they had attracted a small group of interested bystanders. The dog was too wet to put back in the car, so Marjo stood holding him on a leash while he dripped on her feet and Matt single-handedly launched the boat. Halfway through the operation, Flash realized he was wet and shook himself vigorously. Marjo gritted her teeth and hoped none of the onlookers was a potential client for her obedience school.

Matt seemed to know what he was doing with the boat, she noticed with some relief. He had the craft in the water and had handed her the new rope before she had time to reconsider the wisdom of heading out onto the lake with an unruly dog and an unpainted boat. But at least it was floating upright, looking considerably more stable than it had when resting on the trailer.

Matt brought the boat around to the dock and held it while Marjo gingerly climbed in. Flash needed no urging; he leaped off the dock with a bound that set the boat rocking and had Marjo grabbing at the windshield to keep her balance. The dog scrambled up onto the small deck at the bow of the boat and stood wagging his tail and looking out over the smooth surface of the water.

"Might as well leave him up there," Matt commented. "At least he's not dripping on us."

Marjo eyed the muddy footprints on the deck, glanced down at her already damp jeans, and nodded.

She settled onto the passenger side of the bench seat, and Matt climbed in beside her and started the engine. It took a couple of tries, but eventually it coughed to life, and he switched on the running lights, then stood up in front of the seat to steer the small craft out onto the darkening lake.

The shoreline slipped away, the noise of the engine drowning out the sounds of the boat launch and the teenagers at the ice-cream stand. Marjo leaned back against the wooden seat and pulled her zippered Green Bay Packers sweat shirt more closely around her, hunching her shoulders against the cool breeze.

"What did I tell you, Ms. Opaski?" Matt shouted at her over the noise of the engine. "She floats."

There was no question but that they were afloat, headed for an evening of stargazing and . . . whatever . . . and Marjo felt herself smiling, her worries about Opie's moodiness and the kennel's minor problems slipping away. Reality—present and promising reality— was the cool breeze across the smooth, dark surface of the lake, the sound of the engine taking them away from shore, the man beside her. *A new man in her life*.

Matt cut the engine when they were a few hundred yards from shore, and they coasted to a stop in the sudden silence. He sat down beside Marjo and glanced across at her, his profile shadowed in the twilight, while waves lapped gently against the bow and the sounds of the shore carried distantly across the water. She looked back at him, then turned away, pushing down the uncomfortable feeling that he could read her thoughts. Self-consciously, she trailed one hand over the side of the boat. "Oh, my!" She pulled her fingers out of the water, shaking them briskly. "It's cold!"

Matt grinned at her. "It's only May. You expected the tropics?"

Raising her eyebrows in mock disdain, she flicked her fingers at him.

"Hey!" He grabbed her wrist. "That was nasty, Ms. Opaski."

"Well, people who own leaky boats shouldn't make smart-aleck remarks at the passengers."

"Hey—she floats, doesn't she?"

She smirked. "The paint is peeling."

"It's not the paint that holds 'em up."

"Fortunately."

He was still holding her wrist. His thumb brushed across the inside of it, and Marjo felt her pulse leap under that slow, almost absent caress. She fell silent, her smile fading. The first stars were glimmering in a clear sky, and a sliver of moon hovered over the skyline of the city behind them.

"So, here we are, Ms. Opaski." He let go of her wrist and put his arm around Marjo's shoulders.

She leaned her head back against him, taking in the feel of his cotton jacket against the back of her neck, breathing in the faint smell of citrus. "Away from the lights of the city?" she asked. Her voice was a little breathless. There was a familiar catch in her throat. She glanced at Matt's face, inches from her own, sidelit by the lights of Milwaukee, which cast a noticeable glow across the western sky; she could see the stars more clearly, she decided, from her own backyard.

"Mmm," Matt murmured again. "Without the kids."

She was aware, acutely and very physically, that they were here without the kids. That he could, with just a slight movement of his head, touch her mouth with his. That she wanted him to, with the kind of eagerness she hadn't felt since long before her divorce.

Suddenly flustered at her own aggressive yearnings, Marjo tipped her head back and squinted up at the stars. "I think I can find the Big Dipper," she told Matt. "Yes —there it is. And that's the North Star, right?"

"Right. If we know where that is, we can always find our way home."

"In case we lose Milwaukee?"

"Mmm." He grinned at her, his teeth a flash of white in the darkening evening. His jacket was open at the throat. His pulse was beating, faintly, in counterrhythm to her own. "And there—" He pointed with the arm that circled her shoulders, pulling her closer to him as he bent his elbow. "That's the Little Dipper. With the North Star in the handle. And up there"—he tipped his head toward hers—"the little bunch of stars close to-gether—that's the Pleiades, the Seven Sisters. See them?"

"Mmm." She nodded, her head nestled against Matt's shoulder, her attention considerably closer to home than the Pleiades.

"It's supposed to be a good test of your eyesight if you can see all seven of them." He dropped his hand down to Marjo's head and threaded his fingers into the hair at the side of her temple.

She squinted up at the small, whitish blur overhead. "I can only see two."

"Mmm. Yeah, you're right. Maybe it's not dark enough yet."

It was never going to be dark enough. Half of the sky above them was washed with a milky glow from down-town Milwaukee, but that seemed irrelevant when her heart was thumping greedily in her chest, and Matt's fingers were working magic in her hair. "Mmm," she got out.

He turned a little toward her. "Do you know any others?" His breath fanned her cheek as he spoke.

"Any other . . . what?"

The Pleiades were blotted out by Matt's head as he lowered his mouth to hers.

The kiss was slow, sensuous, and addicting. When, after long moments, he moved his mouth across hers to nuzzle her cheek, she turned her head so that their lips met again.

Marjo entwined her fingers in the hair at the nape of Matt's neck, as if to hold him there. His arm came around her back and pressed her against him. She slid down on the seat to fit her body against his.

And then she realized that the toe of her sneaker was immersed in something cold and wet.

"Mmm . . . Matt!"

"What?" he mumbled.

She squirmed back onto the seat, pointing down at the bottom of the boat. "It's leaking! The boat's leaking."

Matt stared down at the half-inch deep puddle at their feet, his arms still around Marjo. "Mmm. I guess so." He pulled her close to him again.

"Matt! You have to *do* something about it!"

"Mmm . . ." He kissed her again, reaching around her legs to pull her feet up onto his lap, out of the water.

"B-but . . ." She hesitated, half kissing him back, not wanting to rebuff his romantic overtures, but at the same time appalled that he was ignoring their situation. "Matt . . . we can't just ignore it, for heaven's sake!" Her voice rose a notch. "We're sinking!"

"But"—he nuzzled her ear—"we're not sinking very fast . . ."

In the darkness, she just caught the telltale glint in his eye. He was teasing her. They were in the middle of Lake Michigan in a sinking boat, and he was teasing her!

"Matt! You said"— her voice rose another notch— "this boat didn't leak!"

"I said she floats," he said reasonably. "I never said she didn't leak a little."

"This is not the time for quibbling."

"You're right. Let's not quibble." His arm around her shoulders pressed her closer.

"Matt! For Pete's sake! Stop grinning!"

Still grinning, he pushed himself up on the seat and unwrapped his arms. "I take it you want to go ashore?"

"Yes."

"Okay. I'll start her up." He stood up at the wheel and reached for the key, whistling a snatch of tune under his breath. She recognized it: "Nearer My God to Thee." The engine coughed once, then started up.

Marjo let out a relieved breath and tucked her feet up under her, her lips curved in a reluctant smile.

Ten seconds later, the engine died. "Damn," Matt muttered.

Marjo's smile died along with the engine, and her back came away from the seat in alarm. In the renewed silence, water lapped against the hull, and Matt's wet sneakers squished gently as he crouched down to examine the ignition.

From the small deck, rhythmic chewing sounds were added to the other sounds. Matt poked his head above the windshield, then bolted upright with another muttered, "Damn!" and a minor splash.

"Flash! Drop it!"

"What does he have?" Marjo asked, peering over the windshield.

"The line for the boat. We won't be able to get it on the trailer without the line. Flash!" He reached for the dog. Flash backed off, the line in his mouth, and lowered his frontquarters, wagging his tail.

"Flash! Dammit, come here!" Matt flung one leg over the windshield and scrambled up onto the deck. The dog sidestepped, backed off again, then made a playful leap to one side. He landed with two feet off the

deck, made a quick, frantic scramble, and with the
scraping of toenails and a magnificent splash, plum-
meted into the lake.

The line snapped neatly at the point where Flash had
been chewing it. Matt grabbed for the windshield as the
boat rocked violently, and the dog, true to his earlier
instincts, started swimming due east, toward the invisi-
ble, far shore, the rope still clutched between his teeth.

Marjo splashed her way to the steering wheel, found
the ignition, and turned the key. The engine started.

"Good girl!" Matt shouted over the noise. He gestured toward the gearshift. "Push it forward. Go ahead
—forward." He gestured again, and Marjo followed his
instructions. The boat kicked into gear. "Now the other
lever . . . right . . . give 'er a little gas."

"Now *what?*" Marjo shouted back.

"Follow that dog! I'll try to grab him."

They chugged slowly toward the swimming dog,
Marjo tentatively at the helm, Matt crouched at the bow,
one hand on the cleat. "A little to lee!" Matt instructed.

"What?" She stood on tiptoe, straining to see around
Matt.

"To lee!" He waved a hand toward his left. Marjo
turned the steering wheel obediently to the left, muttering under the noise of the engine as cold water seeped
between her toes and she strained to catch a glimpse of
Flash at the left side of the boat.

"Matt! I can't see him, for Pete's sake! I don't want
to run him over."

Matt leaned down over the side, reaching. He let go
of the cleat and clutched the frayed end of rope still
attached to it, inching farther over to the side to make a
grab for the dog.

"Matt, for heaven's sake! You'll fall off!" Marjo
shouted, panic in her voice.

"Mmfmmgdmm," he shouted back at her incompre-
hensibly.

The boat lurched. "Got 'im!" Matt yelled up from over the gunwhale, then, "Oh, my God."

"What? What?"

"The rope! It's mmfmmdg the boat!"

"What? What do I do? Matt!"

"Starboard!" he shouted.

Horror-stricken, Marjo leaned toward him, straining to see what was happening. "Which way?"

"Starboard!" Matt bellowed.

She grabbed the steering wheel and jerked it to the left. The boat swung sharply. There was a thump and a lurch, then the frayed rope slipped through Matt's fingers, and he slid from the deck like a wet bass.

The sound he made when he hit the water was spectacular enough to make Marjo's stomach sink in terror and her heart leap into her throat. Panicked and clumsy, she groped for the ignition and shut off the engine, then grabbed the gunwhale and leaned over the side. "Matt! Matt! Are you all right?"

There was no answer but a violent splashing of dog, man, and rope tangled together.

"*Matt!* Where are you?"

"I'm right here!" he shouted back at her. "In the damn lake!"

"Oh, Lord." At his voice, her stomach uncoiled one notch and her heart thumped heavily back into her chest. "Are you all right?"

"Of course I'm not all right. This water is the temperature of liquid nitrogen!"

"Oh—I *told* you you were going to fall off." She made a grab for the nearest life jacket and flung it toward him. There was a thunk as it connected with Matt's forehead, then a gurgle, frantic splashing, and a sputtered, "Dammit!"

"*Matt!*"

"For godsake! Are your trying to drown me?"

"I'm sorry—I can't *see* anything."

"Well, you were right on target, for godsake!"

"Will you stop *swearing?* I'm doing the best I can. It's not my fault you fell in the lake."

"I didn't fall in the lake, you *dumped* me in."

"I did not! You said—"

"I said *starboard*, for godsake!" He shoved the life jacket toward the boat and started an awkward side-stroke after it, towing the dog by the collar.

Marjo leaned over the side of the boat to retrieve the life jacket. She heaved it over the gunwhale and flung it into the back of the boat. It made a small splash as it landed. "How am I supposed to know what starboard means?" she fumed.

"It means *right,*" he growled at her.

"Well, then why didn't you just say right?"

Matt reached the side of the boat, gave a kick and a splash and grabbed for the gunwhale. His fingers slipped off the wet wood. "Damn!"

She leaned over and reached toward him. "Give me your hand. And stop swearing," she snapped.

"Dammit, woman, do you know how cold this water is?"

"Of course I know how cold it is. I'm standing in it! Your damn boat is sinking."

His hand closed around her wrist. She grasped him and yanked back with all her strength. Matt hauled him-self up, dripping and shivering, then pulled up on the rope to tow Flash in against the side of the boat and leaned over to grab him by the front paws. He gave a massive heave, but couldn't pull the dog over the gun-whale.

Without instruction, Marjo grasped the back of his wet belt, braced her feet on either side of him, and pulled back as he gave another try. Flash's front paws cleared the gunwhale, and with a scrabbling of back feet he was in the boat. Marjo sat down hard in the two-inch-deep puddle.

"Are you all right?" Matt asked her.

"Of course I'm not all right! My feel are wet and the seat of my pants is wet and we're—sinking!" Furious, she ignored the hand he held out to her and scrambled up on her own.

"We're not going to s–sink," Matt told her, his voice shaking a little with cold. "As soon as I get the engine going I'll start the pump."

"You have a pump? Why didn't you tell me that?"

"Because you were trying to drown me, for Pete's sake."

"I was *trying* to pull you out!"

"Mmfph." He drew a breath that made his teeth chatter audibly and fumbled with the ignition. Flash crossed in front of him, nosing at the rope Matt still held in one hand. "Here," he said shortly. "You hold the dog and I'll start the engine."

Silently, Marjo sloshed toward the dog, grasped his collar, and pulled him out of the way. He went with no protest; then, with magnificent lack of remorse, shook himself vigorously, head to tail, and grinned up at Marjo, tongue hanging out.

The engine sputtered to life, and Matt shifted into gear. Marjo's feet slipped again on the wet floorboards, and she sat down unceremoniously on the wooden seat. Wet, cold, and furious, she set her mouth into a grim line and stared straight in front of her, while Matt swung them around toward the distant lights of the marina. She'd been right about him the first time she'd met him, she decided. He was arrogant and overconfident and . . . and . . . and cold.

He leaned in front of her to flick a switch that turned on a gurgling pump. His hand shook noticeably. She could see his teeth chattering. She set her own mouth into a pinched line and stared at the lights onshore.

He moved the throttle forward slightly. The water in the boat sloshed toward the stern. Their wake fanned

out behind them, and a frigid breeze accompanied the
boat's movement. Matt sat down on the seat, partially
out of the breeze, and wrapped one arm around his shivering torso. Marjo hunched miserably into her own
damp sweat shirt.

They were both cold and wet, and now he'd be in a
vile mood, and it would all, of course, be her fault. She
swallowed hard against an emotion she didn't want to
acknowledge, holding on to her anger with stubborn determination.

"M—Ms. Opaski?" he said after a moment.

She glanced at him warily.

"I think I've learned s—something tonight."

"Oh?"

He grinned at her in the dark, his smile shaky. "V—
vice in Wisconsin is d—damn cold."

Her mouth dropped open with comically blank surprise. "Oh."

"W—wet, too."

She found herself smiling back at him in the darkness. "Maybe we'd better stick to virtue."

"Oh, I don't think we have to go quite that far." He
glanced across at her again. His hair was plastered
against his head, his wet jacket clung to him in clammy
folds, and he was shivering uncontrollably, but there
was, nonetheless, a glint in his eye that she recognized.

Sudden, breathless laughter bubbled up in her chest.
He was incorrigible. And sexy. And funny. And his
sense of humor disarmed her more quickly than the
most persuasive argument could have done. She grinned
at him. "No, I suppose not."

"M—Marjo?"

"What?"

"It wouldn't be quite so c—cold if we s—sat a little
closer."

She glanced down at her hands, wrapped around
Flash's collar. "All three of us?" she asked archly.

"That dog—" Matt said through gritted and still-chattering teeth, "can swim back to the pound in Chicago, for all I care at the moment."

"I see." She nodded, but for good measure snapped the dog's leash onto his collar and tied it to the center support of the seat, then glanced up at Matt again, smiling.

"Come here," he ordered. He reached one clammy arm around her shoulders and pulled her against his wet side.

He was cold and dripping and he smelled of lake water and wet dog, and she snuggled against him with no protest except her shivering body, until the faint warmth of body heat seeped through their damp clothes.

"Ms. Opaski?" he said again after a moment.

"Yes?"

"I forgive you for dumping me in the lake."

"I did not dump—" Marjo began.

"And for hitting me over the head with a life jacket and trying to drown me," Matt interrupted.

"I did not—" Chuckling, she tried to pull away from him.

His arm dropped from her shoulders to circle her waist, and he worked his icy fingers inside her shirt to warm them on her goose-pimpled skin. "I will even try to warm you up, Ms. Opaski, not to mention saving you from a sinking boat."

Still smiling, she slipped her own cold fingers inside Matt's shirt. He winced at the chilly touch, but made no objection. "How're you going to warm me up when you're freezing yourself?"

"Give me half an hour," he told her. He glanced at her, then grinned again, with boyish, incorrigible intent. "I have a Plan."

CHAPTER EIGHT

THEY GOT THE boat loaded onto the trailer with no additional problems, then sat in the car with the heater running full blast while Matt warmed up enough to stop shivering, and Flash rolled around in the back of the station wagon, shedding wet dog hair on Matt's upholstery.

"Dry clothes," Matt mumbled as he pulled away from the graveled launch area.

"Dry clothes?"

"The Plan calls for dry clothes. And hot coffee. And a fire in the fireplace." He glanced at her. "Let's head for my house."

"Mine's closer."

"Mmm. But I'd never fit into your clothes." He gave her a leer.

She smirked back at him, then looked away. *Hot coffee. And a fire in the fireplace.* Recent, vivid memories of Matt's house and hot coffee and a fire in the fireplace made her pulse thrum a little faster. She swallowed, aware of the urgings of her body, aware, too, that the restraints that had kept her celibate since her divorce were disappearing like so many quarters in a video machine.

Matt wrapped a casual, proprietary arm around her shoulders, pulling her closer to him on the seat, as if it were perfectly natural for him to do so.

A new man in her life. She cast a quick, covert glance at him, taking in the clean profile, the wet hair starting to curl over his ears, the defined ridge of muscle beneath his collarbone, where his wet shirt stuck to his chest. A coil of anticipation tightened in her stomach, warming her insides with something far more potent than coffee—and bringing with it a warning chillier than the water of Lake Michigan. She swallowed again, telling herself that this time *she* would be in control; she would be cautious; she would hang on to her independence no matter what the cost of it.

But the pressure of Matt's protective arm around her shoulders was undeniably welcome, and the pleasure of being wanted felt deliciously good. Without thought beyond her impulses, she slipped her hand between the small of his back and the car seat, and he leaned forward to accommodate her while he snuggled her in closer to him.

The side of her breast was pressed against his wet jacket. Marjo shivered slightly as damp cold seeped through sweat shirt, white cotton blouse, and bra, only to be replaced by warmth that hardened her nipple to a tiny nub of insistent longing.

Matt's hand tightened around her upper arm. "Cold?" he asked her. She shook her head against his shoulder. "No." The word came out breathy and revealingly nervous, and she chuckled self-consciously as she added, "Not now."

Matt glanced down at her face, his mouth curved in the slightest of smiles, then he turned his eyes back to the road, his lips pursed in a silent whistle that left the tune to her imagination.

When they pulled into his driveway a few minutes later, the house was dark except for the yellow glow of the back porch light spilling over the steps and part of the lawn. Marjo gazed at the house in silence, registering the fact that there was no one else home. The nervous coil of anticipation in her stomach tightened another notch. She started to ask where Timmy was, but before she could speak, Matt had opened the car door and slid out, keeping his arm around Marjo's shoulders to pull her with him. She scrambled out beside him under the steering wheel, both of them chuckling at the awkward movement, and he tucked her against his side as he walked around to the back of the car to open the tailgate for his dog.

Flash came bounding out of the car with muddy enthusiasm. "No!" Matt ordered with enough irritation to make the dog's ears droop in apology.

Marjo gave a small, surprised laugh. "Hey—that wasn't bad. There may be hope for you yet as a dog owner."

He grinned down at her. "Just don't forget my other attributes."

She returned his glance, but left his attributes alone as he walked her up the steps. He shivered again in the chilly breeze, his arm around her shoulders as he fumbled one-handed for his house key and opened the door for her.

In the dark hallway, he turned her toward him with sudden, swift intent, and pulled her into his arms as his mouth came down over hers.

The anticipation in her stomach fluttered into desire that sent quivering messages to her breasts as they were pressed against the wet fabric of his jacket, and he held her against him with strong, imperative arms. She clung to him, caught up in the unexpected kiss and in her own swift answering response. Her lips opened to his questing tongue. It was hot, tempting, provocative—and she let it work its spell on her senses, calling up searing desire that defied even her shivering body.

Matt's hands moved down her back to her derriere, pulling her more closely against him as he broke off the kiss. "I just couldn't wait any longer for that," he told her with a husky laugh. "Wet clothes or not."

Her chin was pressed against his shoulder, her body molded against his as he spanned her cold backside with warm hands. She let her eyes slide shut, the better to savor the delight of his hands, his body, the unmistakable ardor with which he held her. It felt irresistible, despite her uncertainties, despite the wet clothes.

Still holding her beside him, he turned to walk her into the kitchen and flick on the lights. "Coffee," he muttered, as if reminding himself of purpose. He released her to cross the room to the coffee maker on the counter.

"Where's Timmy?" she asked, watching him move with quick efficiency in the spare, masculine kitchen, lit only by the dim lamp on the kitchen table. The rest of the house was dark, empty, and silent. The atmosphere of stolen privacy sent a forbidden shiver up her spine.

"He's staying overnight with a friend."

"Oh." She watched him fill the coffee carafe with tap water and pour it into the machine. His wet chinos clung to his backside like a second skin, revealing the solid, muscular contours of buttocks and thighs.

"They're going fishing in the morning, and they want to get up early." Unexpectedly, he turned. The front of his pants was molded to his body as closely as the back, outlining with no disguise the hard ridge of flesh beneath his zipper. Marjo's eyes flew up to his face, and embarrassed color flared in her cheeks.

A ghost of a smile crooked up one corner of his mouth. "I guess it's obvious you turn me on, Ms. Opaski."

Her disconcerted gaze dropped to her feet, and she

wrapped her arms around herself, hugging her elbows as she gave a strained laugh, expecting the kind of sarcastic remark Stan would have made about her being caught looking.

But Matt was silent as he moved a couple of steps toward her, then stopped, hands in his pockets, assessing her defensive posture and downturned gaze.

She cleared her throat. "I . . . ah . . . guess I thought . . . Timmy would be home." Her slight, apologetic smile faded as Matt studied her silently, his own expression unsmiling.

"Do you mind that he's not?"

She drew in a deep breath, then swallowed convulsively, trying to quell the sudden panic of butterflies in her stomach. "I don't know," she said honestly, then dropped her eyes again. "I guess—" She clutched her elbows more tightly, letting out a breath that seemed squeezed from her chest. "I guess I'm just not very used to this. I mean—I was married for years, but—" She broke off again, with an embarrassed laugh, then bit her lip and brought one hand up to her eyes to cover her face. "The last time I made a decision like this I was seventeen. And I made a pretty horrible mess of it."

There was a surprised pause before he asked softly, "There hasn't been anyone since your husband?"

She shook her head.

"Marjo." His fingers closed around her hand, and he tugged it gently away from her face. "We're human. We make mistakes. And we try again."

She lifted uncertain eyes to his. "I don't want to make that kind of mistake again." Her voice was a thin thread of self-doubt as she admitted, "I don't want to—lose control of my life again."

"You think I want to take control of your life?"

"I—no. I just—I don't—"

His hand slipped around her neck to thread into the

hair above her collar. One corner of his mouth lifted in a sketch of a smile. "Don't what?"

"I don't trust myself," she blurted out, her eyes clouded with indecision, her voice shaky. "I don't trust myself not to just—let someone else take over my life. To just give up everything I want . . ."

He pulled her head against his chest, wrapping her in strong arms that cradled her against him. "You don't have to give up anything. Why should you?"

"Because I'm a woman. And that's what I was brought up to think a woman's role should be. To be self-sacrificing and supportive and nurturing and to—to take the blame for everything."

He drew back a little to turn her face toward his, holding it between his hands. "I don't want someone to blame, Marjo," he said quietly. "I want someone to make love to."

She stared back at him, vulnerable and wide-eyed, until he lowered his head to touch his mouth gently to hers, angling it to fit more closely, moving his lips against hers with tantalizingly gentle pressure. He let his hands slide down to her shoulders, then along her upper arms as he drew them around his waist and gathered her against him with a tenderness that coaxed and persuaded, until her lips parted and her hands on his back drew him close.

The kiss sent shivers of sensation radiating out to her whole body, and she yielded to it with the inevitability of winter to spring. Matt's arms around her back tightened, and he pulled her hard against him as with lips and tongue he demanded and claimed what she gave. When he broke off the kiss, his breathing was rough and uneven against the side of her face.

"Dry clothes," he whispered into her ear. He pressed his lips against her cheekbones. "And a fire in the fireplace." He kissed her temple. "And . . . the rest." Purposefully, he drew her head against his shoulder, and turned her slightly to walk her past the fragrant coffee machine into the dark living room.

Flash padded along behind them, smelling of wet dog.

They stopped at the fireplace, where a fire was already laid with crumpled newspapers and logs, and crouched down in front of it. With one hand, Matt took a box of matches off the top of the mantel, and, still with his arms around her, extracted a match from the box and struck it on the brick hearth.

He tossed the match into the fireplace, then turned her toward him to kiss her again as the newspapers caught flame and sent orange lights dancing against her closed eyelids. Still crouched on his heels, Matt brought his hand to the side of her cheek to tip her face into his, fitting his mouth against hers as his tongue coaxed her lips open and slipped inside.

Heat fanned against her shoulder and her arm as the fire licked upward to the logs, and heat of another kind flared through her as Matt's hot, wet tongue met hers. He stood up, again pulling her with him, his hands around her upper arms as they kissed with an urgent thrusting of tongues, the exploration fevered and mutually demanding.

He broke off the kiss with a rasping breath, then pressed his mouth against the side of her neck before he muttered in a voice gruff with barely controlled passion, "God, Marjo, I was going to take it slow . . ." He gave a husky chuckle. "But I don't know what you do to me . . ."

She laughed with him—a breathless sound deep in her throat that betrayed her own shaky control. "Maybe it's known as dumping you in the lake."

He buried his face in her neck again, nuzzling the sensitive cord at the side of her neck as he spoke against her skin. "You have a way of warming me up, woman, that makes it worth the experience." His tantalizing tongue drew lines of liquid fire around to the hollow of her throat as he nudged aside her damp collar. "Anyway," he murmured, "you're almost as wet as I am." He moved his head lower, warming her with his breath as his fingers snaked up to unzip the sweat shirt, then unfasten the top button of her shirt.

She arched her back, lost in pleasure as the heat of his breath replaced the dampness of her wet clothes. His questing mouth moved lower, and she felt his fingers unfasten the next button. She leaned back against his supporting arm, letting him undress her, delighting in the sensation of warmth that replaced the dampness of her clothes.

When her shirt hung open, he straightened again, then circled her neck with his hands, hesitating for a moment before he slid his palms along her collarbone to push shirt and sweat shirt off her shoulders and down her arms. Without moving his eyes from her face, he reached behind him and draped both garments over the half-eaten jade plant.

Welcome heat from the fire touched her arm, her shoulder, then her back, as Matt's hands on her bare shoulders turned her slightly and reached around her to unfasten the clasp of her bra.

He stepped back from her to draw the garment down her arms, then stood for a moment looking at her, his eyes dark and intense as his gaze fell on her uncovered breasts. Marjo crossed her arms across her midriff in a brief, self-conscious gesture; then, slowly, dropped her arms to her side as she met Matt's gaze.

She smiled, with slow, unaffectedly seductive invitation, then reached up for the collar of Matt's jacket. The zipper rasped unevenly as it caught on the wet fabric, and she worked it free with impatient fingers, then started on the lowest button of his shirt, tugging his shirttails out of his damp chinos while he drew in a rough breath. His eyes slid closed as she worked her way up the front of his shirt, unfastening the wet buttons one at a time while he stood unmoving, letting her do as she wished.

His breathing was rapid; the pulse at the hollow of his throat beat in swift, heated tempo. She slipped her hands inside his shirt to the side of his waist, just above his pants, then ran her fingers around to the front of his ribcage, barely touching him, exploring the texture of damp skin, sparse, soft curly hair over hard, defined muscle. Her hands hesitated at the center of his chest, then spread outward so that she covered his nipples with her palms.

Matt shrugged off the wet jacket and shirt with impatient haste and let them drop on the floor behind him. Marjo could feel the slight tremor of his hands as he wrapped them around her again. His skin was warm and damp and smelled of Lake Michigan and citrus. She pressed her mouth to his breastbone, then traced with her lips the hard ridge of muscle that spanned his chest.

"Oh, God, Marjo . . ." he murmured, his voice thick. "You feel . . . so good. But I can't . . ." He bent to capture her mouth again with his, sliding his hands down her back to pull her against him, flattening her bare breasts against his chest as he moved in slow, erotic, back-and-forth motions that abraded her nipples against his hard chest.

She made a low, incoherent sound deep in her throat. Matt's palms spread wide across her shoulder blades, moving and controlling her as he continued to plunder her mouth with his tongue. Erotic currents of pleasure fanned outward from her breasts to the pit of her stomach, her thighs, the silken center of her womanhood.

Doubts and inhibitions evaporated in the heat of passion that had been held too long under rigid control. Her seeking hands slid down his back until she slipped her fingers inside the waistband of his chinos, seeking warm skin beneath the wet fabric. Her fingers traced the inside waistband around to the honed, hard flesh above his hipbones, and he sucked in his breath as her hands continued their path around to the front of his chinos. She tugged at the snap impatiently, her own urgency as great as his to touch, to learn, to claim.

Matt let his head fall back, his hands resting lightly on her shoulders, letting her set the pace, taking fervent pleasure in her eagerness, but when her hand closed around the shaft of his manhood, warm, stroking, erotic, he groaned deep in his throat and moved his hand over hers to stop her.

"I can't hold off, if you do that," he gasped, his voice thick.

With one movement, he scooped her up in his arms and across the living room, through the dark hallway, and into a bedroom lit only by shadowy bars of moonlight filtered through a light colored, transparent curtain. Flash padded after them, nosing into the bedroom at Matt's heels.

"Stay," Matt muttered to the dog, then kicked the bedroom door shut with one foot, leaving Flash outside, shutting himself and Marjo into shadowy darkness. The bedspread, as he lowered her onto it, was some cool silky material, and she shivered slightly as it touched her back and shoulders.

Matt leaned over her to touch his warm mouth to the hollow of her neck and shoulder, as she felt his fingers unsnap and unzip her jeans. Unable to lie still, needing the feel of warm skin against hers, she reached for the snap of his chinos. Insistently, she worked the trousers down over his hips.

The mattress sagged as he sat on it to oblige her by pulling the wet pants off and dropping them on the floor. Then he reached for her again, copying her actions, pulling off denim jeans and silky underpants in one motion.

His breath was strident and rushed in the quiet of the

bedroom, but his hands, cupping her hips and stroking up to the curve of her waist, were languid and agonizingly slow as they feathered over her ribs, then inched higher to trace the undercurve of her breasts with fingertips that barely touched her skin but sent shivery, electric currents of sensation to the hardened peaks. He cupped the outer sides of her breasts in his palms, cradling and caressing while she arched her back to him, her breath suspended in her throat as she waited, achingly impatient, for his full touch.

He bent his head toward her in the darkness, and his warm, wet mouth closed around one hardened nipple. The breath came out of her lungs in a rush of half-audible passion. She clung to him, lost in sensation, aware only of pleasure given and taken with all-consuming concentration.

His mouth moved to her other breast, working electric torment with his lips and tongue, sending currents of desire all through her body. Barely conscious of her actions, she raised one knee and rolled slightly toward him, while her hands sought his hips and her fingers curved into the muscles of his buttocks, urging him toward the yearning center of her body.

He made a sound of inarticulate desire deep in his throat as he hitched one knee up beside her hips and turned in response to her demand. She moved her hand to reach for him, stroking his velvet hardness, urging him toward her.

With one swift movement, he was leaning over her, supporting his weight on his elbows, his fingers threaded into her hair as he sought her mouth with his. His breath came harsh and fervent; his mouth plundered hers with fierce possession as he thrust into her body with barely controlled power.

But control was not what she wanted, pace and measure not what she craved. Her fingers clenched into the hard muscles of his buttocks. Her hips surged up to meet his thrust, to claim his possession, and together, beat for beat, they rode toward imminent, impending ecstasy, the tempo wild and rushed, until their release quickened and exploded in shimmering circles. She gave a cry of incoherent, elemental pleasure that was caught and returned by her lover.

Matt held her hard against him, his hand cradling the back of her head, his face buried in her neck. Slowly, his trembling muscles relaxed, and he rolled onto his side and slid his arm under Marjo's shoulders to pull her with him. She turned toward him, one hand still resting on his buttocks while her breathing slowed and she drew sensuous, lethargic circles against his skin with the palm of her hand.

Outside the bedroom door, there was a subdued snuffling, then a sigh and the sound of a canine body being slumped against the threshold.

Gradually, Marjo's hand stilled and then withdrew, as perception trickled back to her. Her fingers fluttered timidly on Matt's hip for an instant, then she tucked her arm against her chest, fingers curled loosely under her chin.

In the dark, his hand groped for hers, closed warmly around it, and replaced it on his backside. "Do that some more," he muttered gruffly. "I like it."

She gave a burst of abashed laughter. "I didn't want you to think I was . . . too aggressive."

There was a rustle of smooth bedspread as he raised himself on one elbow, then his fingers threaded into her hair again with fierce tenderness. "I think you're womanly and sexy and beautiful, sweetheart. Don't ever change that."

She laughed again, lightly brushing her palm against his skin. "As long as you don't mind . . . demanding women."

A deep chuckle rumbled in his chest, and he pulled

her half on top of him, rolling onto his back. "Sweetheart, you can have me any time you want me."

She laughed with him, light-hearted laughter that bubbled up from deep inside, in a current of pure, unstifled pleasure.

"Any time?" she teased, moving her hand around to the front of his body.

He caught her hand in his and returned it to its place. "Any *reasonable* time, woman!" He chuckled. "I'm not Superman."

She smiled into his shoulder. "Maybe I could ply you with coffee?"

He turned his face toward hers and she felt his grin. "I think," he said solemnly, "it's definitely worth a try."

The sun was high in the morning sky, slanting in through the bedroom curtains onto the maroon bedspread when Matt opened his eyes. One corner of the sunlit square touched Marjo's blonde curls, strewn across his shoulder where her head was pillowed on his arm. With his free hand, he reached up to stroke a lock of hair. It had the texture of warm silk. She was sleeping like a child, snuggled against him, one arm thrown over her head with the fingers curled loosely in a fist. She looked young, vulnerable . . . virginal.

His index finger traced the silky curl again. She had been . . . a surprise. The kind of sensuous, uninhibited lover a man dreamed about. His mouth curved in a slow smile. A lion-tamer with freckles.

He closed his fingers to brush the back of his knuckles against her hair. The lion-tamer had made a sudden appearance, he knew. He'd half expected her to back off again, half resigned himself to another cold shower and involuntarily extended patience.

But last night the cold shower hadn't been necessary.

The corners of his mouth turned up again. The coffee hadn't been necessary, either.

He glanced at the clock on the bedside table. Nine-fifteen. He should wake her up. She might have an early lesson. He reached for her shoulder, but stopped short of touching her, instead raising himself on one elbow to gaze down at her sleeping face. He didn't want to wake her up, he realized.

His mouth quirked ironically at one corner. He didn't want to wake her up because he wasn't sure, in the bright light of day, what her reaction would be. And he didn't want to go back to cold showers.

His gaze fell on her bare shoulder, then moved up to the golden spill of hair on the pillow. He didn't want to lose her. He let his breath out with a sudden exhalation that he felt all the way to the pit of his stomach. *He very much didn't want to lose her.*

Marjo stirred, turned her head against his shoulder, and opened her eyes. He watched her startled gaze flick once around the room, then back to his face, then she smiled up at him, her blue eyes sleepy, innocent, and trusting.

The small knot of tension in his stomach relaxed.

He smiled back at her. "Morning."

"Morning." She rubbed a fist across her eyes, then rested her wrist on her forehead, blinking. "What time is it?"

"Nine-fifteen." He grinned. "Time for some coffee, I think."

"Coffee, huh?" she mumbled, her voice still husky with sleep. She reached out to trail languid fingers down his arm.

Still grinning, he rolled over to trap her shoulders between his elbows, threaded his hands into her hair, and kissed her. "Yes," he murmured against her mouth. "Coffee."

She linked her arms around his shoulders. Her mouth opened to his to return the kiss.

A moment later, he raised his head a few inches and

brushed a lock of hair away from her temple. "No regrets, Ms. Opaski?"

She shook her head, the blue eyes wide.

"Good. I was"—his fingers stroked through her hair, gentle and sensuous—"afraid you'd change your mind."

Behind his shoulders, she linked her hands together with sudden, fierce possessiveness. "No," she said vehemently, then, as if aware that she'd betrayed more feeling than she'd expected, she repeated more softly, "No."

His fingers fell still, and he studied her for a moment in silence, then a slight smile curved his mouth. "You surprised me last night, Ms. Opaski. I didn't expect . . . a lion-tamer." He lowered his head toward hers again, but she turned aside with sudden sharpness. He stopped, looking faintly startled at the unexpected gesture. She gave a self-conscious cough. "I—I'm not usually—I mean—"

"What?"

A wash of color rose in her cheeks. "Well, I know that a man expects to . . . to do the pursuing."

"Hey—" He turned her face toward his. "For a liberated lady, you have some pretty old-fashioned notions, Ms. Opaski."

Her eyelids fluttered down diffidently. "A lot of men are . . . old-fashioned."

"Well, a lot of us aren't. And anyone who told you you had to be submissive and retiring was—" He broke off, then his mouth hardened. "—was wrong."

She sketched a tremulous smile, ill-at-ease with the intimate conversation. "I guess I'm not used to . . . not being wrong."

"I'm not him, Marjo," he said intently. "And you're not a seventeen-year-old who has to take all the blame for a mistake that wasn't all yours."

"I—I know." She swallowed, then linked her fingers more tightly behind his neck, but she turned her head away from him as she repeated, with a trace of bitterness, "That part of my life is over."

Matt's dark eyes studied her averted face for a moment, then his palm slipped under her cheek and he turned her head back toward him, the movement gentle but insistent. "I'm not him," he said again.

Marjo met his gaze, her own eyes serious, still half-haunted by doubt but not leaving his face as she took in every detail: dark eyes, straight nose, expressive, beguiling mouth. Her hands moved behind his shoulders to clasp the back of his head, and her lips parted in half-conscious invitation. *A new man in her life.* "Matt," she said softly. "I want—"

His eyes grew infinitesimally darker. "What do you want?" he said finally.

Watching him, she said steadily, "I want you to make love to me again."

By infinitely slow degrees, he lowered his mouth to hers to answer her bidding.

The taste of Matt's mouth was still on hers, the memory of his lovemaking imprinted on her mind, when she dismissed her Sunday morning obedience class two hours later. In the confusion of dogs and clients sorting themselves out in her parking lot, Marjo didn't see Opie and her grandmother drive in until Opie had come bounding out of the car, slamming the door behind her.

"Mom! I'm home!" The girl came running across the gravel parking lot, dodging dogs and waving hurried greetings to their owners. She was carrying a shoebox-sized package, holding it in front of her as she ran.

"Hi, honey." Marjo gave her daughter a hug, then ruffled her blonde curls and grinned at her. "Did you have a good time? What have you got there?"

"It's a present!" Opie snatched the top off the shoebox and pushed aside the white tissue paper over a pair of pink slippers made of some plastic material. "From Dad!"

Marjo froze where she was, while Opie snatched one of the shoes out of the box and held it up happily for her mother's inspection.

"Jellies," the girl bubbled. "Aren't they awesome? And Dad might come for a visit! He said he might come!"

Marjo stared at the pink plastic shoe in her daughter's hand, her frozen smile disintegrating like cracking porcelain, while something cold crept up from the pit of her stomach to the back of her throat.

"They fit perfectly!" Opie went on, turning the shoe over in her hand, entranced with the gift. "Dad found out my size from Gram. They came yesterday in the mail!"

"In the mail?" Marjo's voice was squeezed through muscles in her throat that seemed paralyzed.

"Yeah." At the strained tone of her mother's voice, Opie glanced up from the shoes. The girl's excited, barely containable smile faltered. "The package came by overnight express."

"Oh." Marjo swallowed hard and nodded. Carefully, she removed her arm from Opie's shoulder. Staring at the pink plastic shoes, she twisted her hands together in front of her, as if to control an impulse too strong to be trusted.

"I was really..." At the sight of her mother's white face, Opie's smile faded into an expression of uncertainty, then she gave a small, self-conscious shrug and finished, "I was really surprised."

"Well that's—nice, honey." She couldn't seem to breathe through her constricted throat. The words were a thin, unnatural squeak.

Opie's blue eyes, fixed on her mother's, widened in hurt confusion, then her gaze dropped to the shoe in her hand. "I was just...really surprised," she mumbled again, her eyes downcast. She hesitated, then put the shoe back in the box and replaced the cover.

Marjo's heart contracted with guilty pain as the last of Opie's enthusiasm drained away. "Honey—I–I'm glad you liked your present," she managed. "Did you—thank your grandmother for having you overnight, Opie?"

"Uh—no," Opie muttered. She turned to walk with dragging feet toward her grandmother. Marjo followed, deliberately unclasping her hands to push them into her pockets.

The small, plump figure of Anna Wozniak, in a flowered dress, was standing beside the car as they approached. She leaned down to give the girl a hug, then straightened to smile at Marjo. The expression on the pleasant, blue-eyed face was a little anxious as her glance skittered from Marjo's pinched face to the box in Opie's hands, but she patted Opie's shoulder with the long-standing concern of a protective grandparent who would not bring up difficult questions in front of a child. "We had a good weekend, didn't we, Opie?" she murmured.

The girl glanced at her mother, then nodded half-heartedly.

"That's—nice, honey." Guilt twisted through Marjo's insides, but she couldn't manage the other woman's pat smile.

"The package came as quite a surprise to all of us," Opie's grandmother continued, with a quick glance at Marjo, "but wasn't it lucky that Opie was staying with us overnight, so she could be there to get the present from her father?"

"Yes . . . lucky," Marjo said faintly. She nodded, feeling numb, trying to push back the thought of why Opie had been staying overnight with her grandparents. Oh, Lord, where had *she* been, what had *she* been doing while Opie was getting presents from her father?

"Opie was so excited—" Stan's mother broke off, then patted the girl's shoulder once more. "I've never seen her so pleased with a present."

Opie's confused, unhappy gaze moved from her mother to her grandmother, then her chin tipped at a mutinous angle and her mouth trembled dangerously. "It's not such a big deal!" she flung out at them. "It's just a—dumb pair of shoes!" She spun on her heel and ran toward the house, the box tucked under her arm.

"Opie!" Marjo cast a distracted glance at Opie's grandmother, muttered a hurried, "I'm sorry, Anna," and dashed after her daughter, Anna Wozniak's dismayed reassurance following her like a tiny, ineffective flutter of torn paper.

CHAPTER NINE

THE DOOR TO Opie's room was shut tight when Marjo ran up the stairs, her heart pounding in her throat. She stopped in front of her daughter's room, her hand raised to knock, but instead she pressed her fingers against her mouth as if to summon up the right words. Her eyes slid shut in agonized uncertainty for a long moment before she raised her hand and rapped tentatively on the wooden panel.

"Opie?"

She waited, listening to silence on the other side of the door.

She knocked again. "Honey?"

There was another empty pause, then the creak of bedsprings and the shuffle of stockinged feet toward the door.

Opie pulled it open and stood with one hand resting on the doorknob, her weight slung nonchalantly on one hip, her shoulders stiff with belligerence. Her face was carefully—and unnaturally—blank. "Yes?" the girl asked.

"Are you . . . all right, honey?"

Opie stared back at her, then shrugged with studied casualness. "'Course. Why wouldn't I be?"

"Well, I—I just thought—"

"I'm fine, Mom. I was just putting my stuff away."

Marjo's glance flicked around the room. The shoe-box was shoved half under the bed, its cover askew, as if it had been carelessly kicked. "Opie, I—" She took another breath. "I didn't mean to make you feel upset—about the shoes."

Opie's glance wavered momentarily, then her mouth set into a hard line and she glanced back at her mother. "It's no big deal, Mom."

Marjo half reached toward her, palm upward, but her daughter stiffened away. Shocked and hurt, she dropped her hand to her side, then, awkwardly, pushed it into her pocket. "Opie . . ." She tried to make the girl meet her eyes, but Opie's gaze skittered off across the room, avoiding her mother's troubled expression.

"Honey—about what you said about your—your father visiting." Marjo took a breath that didn't seem to fill her lungs, but went on doggedly, "Sometimes—sometimes people say things—you know, just—"

"You don't have to talk about this, Mom." The girl let go of the door, then crossed her room with quick, jerky steps and threw herself onto her bed. She reached for a magazine from the bedside table.

"I don't mind talking about—your father."

Opie gave her a look of palpable disbelief that stopped Marjo in mid-sentence. "I told you, it's no big deal. Anyway, I don't want to talk about it any more than you do. So why don't we just drop it, okay?"

Marjo stood silent, taken aback by the casual tone of defiance that was far too worldly for her ten-year-old. Yet Opie looked as if she meant it. Marjo swallowed down the anxious fear in her throat. Opie couldn't be so—so cynical—as to have learned to put on an act like this, could she? Or was that something else that Marjo had to answer for?

Opie flipped a page of her magazine, with a studied lack of interest in their conversation, then she glanced at her mother again. "Did you have a good time with Matt? In the boat?"

To Marjo's overwrought emotions, the words rang with accusation. Irrational guilt stabbed through her as she gave a slight, barely discernible nod and muttered, "Yes."

Opie turned again to her magazine.

Marjo stood trying to think of another opening to conversation, but nothing came to her. She felt lost and alone, utterly incapable as a parent, utterly unable to fathom Opie's closed, resistant behavior.

The ring of the telephone broke into the strained silence. Marjo's head turned automatically toward it, then she glanced back at Opie. The girl ignored both the phone and her mother.

At the third ring, Marjo let her shoulders slump and moved toward it. She picked up the receiver and muttered a distracted, "Hello."

"Hello yourself. How's the lion-taming business?"

Marjo let out her breath in a rush as she clutched the phone more tightly between her fingers. "Matt." Her voice was as tight as the grip that held the receiver. "How are you?" she got out.

There was a puzzled silence on the other end of the line. "That's what I just asked you."

"Oh. Yes—I'm fi—" But the phrase stuck in her throat. She let her words trail off as her eyes squeezed shut.

"Marjo? What is it?"

The concern in his voice stirred a torrent of emotion that was too precariously close to the edge. "I can't talk now." She swallowed. "I'm sorry."

"Marjo, what's the matter? Is it Opie?"

Marjo's gaze flew back to Opie's door. She said nothing, but she knew all too well the churning, unfocused sense of guilt that held her in an old, familiar grip.

"Look—I'll come over. I know we have a lesson at five o'clock, but—"

"No. I—I think I'll have to cancel today's lesson . . ."

"Marjo, what the hell is going on?"

"I—I'll explain it later. It—has nothing to do with —with us."

"The hell it doesn't!" She heard a sharp intake of breath, then Matt's voice, low and terse, demanded, "Do you have a lesson now?"

"No."

"Then I'm coming over. I'll be there in twenty minutes."

"Matt—"

But the phone had gone dead, the dial tone ringing in her ear in inanimate reproof.

Twenty minutes later, the slam of a car door and the purposeful crunch of footsteps on the gravel broadcast his arrival. There was a hurried knock; then, without waiting for an answer, Matt pulled open the door and took the steps two at a time.

At the top of the landing, he stopped, his hands jammed into his pockets, his shoulders hunched with worry as he gazed at Marjo, standing silently in the front hallway. He let his eyes rove over her in questioning appraisal. When she didn't speak, he said, "Look— I apologize if this is a bad time for me to be here but—" He let out a pent-up explosion of breath. "Dammit, I was worried about you."

Her chin wobbled as two quick tears sprang to the corners of her eyes, and she took half a step toward him.

"Marjo—" He reached for her and gathered her

against him, leaning back against the doorjamb while he cradled her like a child, his arm around her back and one hand nestling her head against his shoulder while he rocked her gently back and forth. "What is it?"

She swallowed the lump in her throat. "Opie got a present from her father," she told him in a choked voice. "And he says he's coming for a visit, and I c– can't... explain..."

"Oh, God." Matt let out a long sigh as he tilted his head down to hers. "God, I didn't know what—"

He lifted his head, then, abruptly, broke off. His arms, around Marjo, loosened, and he straightened away from the doorjamb.

Unwillingly, he released her. "Opie," he murmured. "Hi."

"Hi."

Marjo spun around to face her daughter.

The girl regarded them solemnly while Matt rested his hands on Marjo's shoulders. He gave Opie a slow smile.

The corners of the girl's mouth tipped up tentatively.

"So you got a present," he said.

Opie's smile disappeared, and her gaze dropped to the floor. She shifted her weight to one foot, then the other, and pushed her hands into her pockets. "I think I'll... uh... go check on the dogs," she announced. She walked by them out the door, her gaze on her feet.

Matt watched her go, with no comment beyond a questioning frown, but his hands, on Marjo's shoulders, tightened reassuringly.

The door shut behind Opie. A long sigh lifted Marjo's shoulders under Matt's hands, then they slumped dejectedly as she let her head fall forward and wrapped her arms around herself. "She came home all excited about getting the shoes. And I tried to—to—"

"Pretend it was okay?"

She nodded.

"But Opie knew you didn't approve."

"It's not that I don't *approve*," she said defensively, spinning around to face him. "I just don't want her hurt!"

Matt regarded her with a troubled expression that offered sympathy, but not, it seemed, a full measure of agreement.

"He can't be trusted!" Marjo blurted out. "He'll just —charm her with presents and flowers and promises. He'll get her hopes up, and then he'll disappear again." She shook her head, as if to shake off unacceptable truths. "And I don't know how to tell her that!"

"Maybe you can't."

Marjo looked up at him in surprise and bewilderment.

"Maybe nobody can tell a child that someone she loves is untrustworthy."

"She doesn't l–love him!" She stumbled over the word as if it stuck on her tongue.

Matt said nothing, but his gaze dropped from hers and one hand came up to rub the back of his neck.

"We haven't heard from him in three years," she went on. "He was out of our lives!" She gestured in the air, distraught. "It's not fair! Why should he have to do this *now?*"

Matt's hand dropped from his neck. "Maybe Opie contacted *him*, Marjo. Maybe she wrote him a letter or called him or something."

Marjo stared at him, then shook her head in disbelief. "No. No, Opie wouldn't do that. She couldn't have done that."

"Why don't you ask her?"

"No." She shook her head again, vehemently.

"Why not?"

"I don't . . ." She faltered. "I don't want to put the thought in her head. I—don't want to bring up the subject."

Matt's gaze held hers steadily.

"It wouldn't do any good to talk about it anyway! It wouldn't change anything about him! He'd still be the same kind of man! Full of promises"—She half turned away from Matt, wrapping her arms around herself again—"but never there when you need him."

There was a short, shocked silence, then he said, with an edge to his voice, "Have you needed him a lot lately?"

She spun around again to face him with a pointed, defensive stare. *"I just don't want Opie upset.* She has a lot of unresolved feelings about him—"

"She has a lot of unresolved feelings?"

Marjo's jaw clenched antagonistically, and she tipped her chin up at a belligerent angle. "I don't have any feelings about him at all."

"No?"

"No!"

He stared back at her, his mouth set. "Then how come I'm talking to a woman I made love to last night and the subject of the conversation is her ex-husband?" he asked, his voice terse.

"We're—I—I'm talking about Opie's father."

"He also happens to have been your husband, Marjo."

"Not anymore. He's not part of my life anymore! I won't let him be part of our lives again!" At her sides, her hands closed into fists.

"Do you think you can shut him out of Opie's life, too? He's her father. You can't change that."

"He gave up his right to be a father! He's not—" She broke off, glaring at Matt, then spouted, "You don't understand any of this!"

"Maybe not. But I'm beginning to understand why it's been three years and there hasn't been any other man. You're still too involved with the first one."

"I'm involved with my daughter and my kennel and my own life!"

There was a flash of hurt behind the anger in the dark eyes that gazed back at her, then he said softly, "And that's all?"

"I—that's not what I meant."

But in a sense, she knew, it had been. She wouldn't let her life be taken over again. Never again. Nothing was going to threaten her independence, or Opie's happiness. And if that made her hard and uncaring, so be it.

A lump of confusing, too-vulnerable emotion was rising in her throat, bringing a sharp, lonely ache to her chest, but she swallowed it down, refusing to give up the anger that was all that was keeping her together.

Matt stood unmoving for what seemed to be an interminable length of time, waiting for her to speak, while it seemed she could feel the same ache of emotion from him, then he pushed his hands slowly into his pockets. His eyes held poignant, hurt disillusionment as they rested on her for a long moment. "When you figure out what you meant, let me know," he said finally.

He turned to walk down the stairs, then he was gone. The click of the door seemed to hang like a condemnation in the empty house.

Marjo refused to let herself cry. There was a hard lump of emotion that seemed permanently lodged in her chest as Monday slipped into Tuesday and then Wednesday. But she'd learned her lesson from bitter and inexorable experience: All the tears in the world couldn't change one fact of life. Or buy the groceries or pay the bills.

Or bring back a man who had walked out.

Again and again she told herself she would call Matt; that he wasn't Stan; that he hadn't abandoned her, that it was she who had sent him away. Yet as she'd always done in the years when it had been Stan who'd left, she found herself waiting for Matt to make the first move, to call her, to decide to come back.

On Wednesday night, she came upstairs from her evening class to a ringing phone, and her heart thrummed erratically in her chest as she hurried across the kitchen to reach for it. "Hello?" she offered breathlessly.

"Hello? Jo-Jo?"

The voice on the other end of the line, like an old, destructive habit, reached over three years of her life as if those years had never existed. She backed up against the wall and slid down to the floor like a puppet whose strings had been cut.

"Stan," she muttered faintly.

"Yeah." There was a drawn out, silent pause, then he said, "It's been a long time."

Marjo stared blankly, unspeaking, at the opposite wall of her kitchen, while old feelings washed over her with the force of a tidal wave: incredulity, resentment, the sense that she was powerless to halt what was happening.

"Yes," she finally got out. "A long time."

He cleared his throat. "How're you doin'?"

She could picture the flash of a grin, the boyish charm that he had always counted on to win her over. Had he ever had any doubts that he could?

She didn't answer for a few seconds, while some deep, unyielding core of refusal hardened in her chest. "What—where are you calling from?" she asked.

"My folks' house. I'm here for a few days."

"In Milwaukee?"

"Yeah."

Marjo let out a shocked breath, but said nothing.

"My folks do live in Milwaukee, you know," he said, his tone faintly reproachful.

"I didn't think you ever saw them."

"I've been back every few months to see them," he

told her. "I care about my family, Jo-Jo. Did you think I'd just turn my back on them for three years?"

Silence hummed on the line while in Marjo's head the word *yes* hung heavy with accusation. *Yes, she had every reason to think that he would turn his back on his family.*

"Look—I never called you because I thought—well—" His voice dropped. "I felt guilty as hell about not sending any of the child support. And I thought you wouldn't want me to call."

So why was he calling now? Marjo sat silent, feeling small and hard at her silence in the face of the half-apology. But there was something as hard as granite inside her that resisted giving even an inch.

He cleared his throat once more. "Did Opie—ah—like the shoes?"

"You don't have to buy her presents," Marjo said tightly. "The kennel's doing pretty well. I can afford to buy her all the presents she needs."

There was a hiss of indrawn breath, then a long, deflated sigh before he said softly, "Yeah, I always knew you'd do just fine on your own." He gave a huff of laughter that held no humor. "You were always a hell of a lot stronger than me, Jo-Jo."

"I didn't have any choice," she said tersely.

"Yeah." There was another silence, another sigh before he said, "Yeah, well, I know I wasn't much of a husband or—or father. Hell," he added defensively, "I wasn't much more than a kid myself. But I've done some growing up since then, Jo-Jo." He took another breath. "I've had a pretty good job for the past year and a half. I'm making a little money."

She gripped the phone to her ear, staring at her kitchen cabinets, but seeing in her mind's eye the image of Stan, in the doorway of the fourth floor, one-bedroom South Milwaukee apartment she and Opie had shared for six lean months without him. He'd had a bouquet of red roses in one hand, a gold foil-wrapped present for Opie in the other. His blond hair had been falling across his forehead in the way that had always, in the good times, made her want to reach up to brush it back. She hadn't, at that moment, wanted to touch it. She couldn't imagine ever wanting to touch it.

She said finally, reluctantly, "Opie said you were working as a D.J."

"Yeah. Yeah, I really like the work."

She could picture the boyish grin again, the easy charm that had made her believe him so many times before. "That's—good," she said cautiously, knowing what he was leading up to. She didn't want to hear it.

He cleared his throat again. "I'd—ah—like to see Opie, while I'm here. I thought maybe I could take her to the zoo—"

"No!" Her back came away from the wall as her free hand tightened around the phone cord.

There was a surprised silence, then he said, "Look, I just want to—"

"No. I don't want her to see you."

"Jo-Jo, I know—"

"Don't call me that! My name is Marjo."

"All right! Marjo, then. I just want to take my daughter to the zoo."

"And then what?"

"What do you mean?"

"Then what? You disappear again? You walk out and leave her a note?"

"Look, I—I don't have any definite plans, all right? I don't know how often I'll be back here. We'll just—take it as it comes, all right?"

"I don't want you to see her!"

"Yeah, well, maybe you don't—" He broke off the sharp words, then controlled his voice with an obvious effort. "Marjo—"

"It's been three years!" she cut him off. "She's gotten

used to things the way they are. She doesn't need any changes now, and there aren't going to be any, because that's what's best for Opie!"

"Well, I want what's best for her, too!" Stan's voice rose on a note of anger, then, as before, he controlled it. "For three years, I didn't call, because I figured maybe that *was* what was best for her," he went on, "but when I got her letter it made me do a little rethinking. And maybe there *are* a lot of changes going on now, with your new *boyfriend* and everything—"

"W–What?"

He didn't hear the half-whispered, shocked word. "But Opie's right. He's not her father. I am. And I'm not going to have some other guy standing in for me like I don't even exist."

She stared at the table leg in front of her, stunned into immobility. "What letter?" was all she could squeeze out through her constricted throat.

"The one she wrote to me a month ago." She heard a distant rustle of paper. "April second." There was a pause. "You didn't know about that?"

April second. The day after they had gone out for pizza and video games. When Opie had insisted that she didn't need a new father. Marjo's eyes squeezed shut. The word *boyfriend* grated on her nerves with an intensity that made her stomach weak and left her defenseless against a wave of sick guilt. *Opie* had written to her father. Opie had set this in motion. And Opie was the one who would be hurt again.

But it was Marjo's fault.

No. Her stomach churned with anger. She willed away the sense of helplessness. No, she wouldn't let this happen again.

"No." She said it aloud.

"Oh. I thought you must have known—"

"No, you can't see her."

"Marjo, I—"

"No! I won't have her hurt again!" Her voice rose in desperately unleashed rage. "And if you care about her at all, you won't try to contact her again!"

"Marjo, listen, we're going to at least talk—"

But Marjo had leaped to her feet and slammed the receiver down onto its hook, cutting off his voice with violent finality.

She raised one shaking hand to her forehead, then covered it with the other as she leaned her elbows against the wall beside the phone and closed her eyes. Her whole body trembled uncontrollably as she gulped in air that didn't seem to fill her lungs, and her tangled emotions churned inside her with gut-wrenching opposition.

Opie had written to her father because Marjo had gotten involved with Matt. And she hadn't suspected. Hadn't taken Opie's feelings seriously, because she herself had been too in love with Matt to—

She bit down on her lip to cut off the thought before she finished it, and to cut off with it the unbearable burden of guilt and hurt and that went with it.

In love with him. But the phrase whirled around in her mind as if taunting her with its seductive power. As if it had been waiting there in the back of her mind, though she hadn't used it consciously.

In love with him. She buried her face in her hands as an ache of something so sharply painful it terrified her rose from the middle of her chest to the back of her throat.

Desperately, she swallowed it down. She'd been in love with Stan once. It was one of the weapons he'd used to manipulate her, to play on her feelings of guilt and obligation, and to convince her to try again, over and over. To give up whatever job she'd managed to find, to give up whatever small apartment she could afford—and to be abandoned again—with no job and

no money and no way to explain to her six-year-old
daughter why Daddy had left them.

The door at the bottom of the stairs swung open, and
at the sound of Opie's footsteps on the lower steps
Marjo pushed herself away from the wall and crossed
the kitchen to the counter to busy herself with the first
task that came to mind—anything to give her an excuse
not to face Opie.

"Hi," Opie muttered casually at the top landing.

"Hi, honey." She didn't trust her voice to say more.
She pulled down the dishwasher and reached into it for
one of the clean supper dishes. Her hand shook as she
opened a cabinet to put the dish away.

Opie was watching her curiously from the top of the
stairs, and Marjo took a breath, then turned to look at
her daughter.

Opie had put on one of her mother's sweat shirts
before the lesson had started; it hung loose on her
shoulders, the hem covering the pockets of her faded
jeans. The toe of one sneaker was scuffed with dirt, and
a smudge of dirt slashed across the front of the sweat
shirt, where Opie, like the child she was, had carelessly
wiped one dusty hand. Her blond curls were tousled and
unkempt. She looked young, innocent, and heartbreak-
ingly vulnerable.

Could she still care so much about the father who had
abandoned her so often—who had hurt her so many
times in the past? Marjo bit her lip, not wanting to believe it, but something in her chest contracted painfully
at the thought that Opie had written to her father, and
then had kept the secret for weeks. Why couldn't she
have told her mother what she was thinking? Or had she
felt . . . betrayed?

Marjo clutched at the dish in her hands as she turned
back to the counter, shaken by the reality that the close-
ness between mother and daughter she had always taken
for granted had been breached by a wedge she'd made

herself. And she hadn't realized it. She hadn't wanted to realize it, because she'd wanted, deep in her heart, to believe she could have it all. Her daughter, her work . . . Matt.

The thought of him brought pain to her throat, and the ache of threatened tears to her eyes. She forced them back with strength born of desperation.

"I looked in on the dogs, Mom. They're all okay."

"Th–thank you, honey."

Opie's steps took her into the living room, and a moment later Marjo heard the TV.

She set the plate on the counter, then turned and moved silently to the doorway, where she stood looking in at Opie, slouched on the couch with only the back of her head and one knee showing.

There was no real choice to be made. Opie was the center of her life. Opie was all that really mattered.

All that mattered?

She shut out the lonely cry that seemed torn from her soul, and turned back to the phone. She looked up Matt's number, fighting the protest that seemed like a fresh wound in her heart. She dialed two digits, then stopped. Her eyes squeezed shut. She couldn't talk to him. She wasn't strong enough for that.

There was note paper and a pen in the kitchen drawer. She pulled out the stationery and wrote the note, trying not to think about what Matt's reaction to it would be as she explained in stark and businesslike terms that she was canceling their lessons, and that she thought it was best if they didn't see each other again. She hesitated over the words, *I'm sorry,* but even that simple phrase was too dangerously personal. Her eyes burned with threatened tears as she stared at the paper, and she couldn't bring herself to write the words. She signed it simply, starkly, *Marjo*.

* * *

Stan called twice more late Wednesday night. Both
times Marjo hung up on him. Thursday morning she
found a message on the Opaski Kennels' answering machine saying that he simply wanted to talk to her and
asking her to call him back. She ignored it. The calls
ceased after that, but Marjo hovered near the phone
when Opie was in the house, inventing excuses to stay
in the kitchen until she thought she'd go mad staring at
the four walls of the small room.

Friday evening, when the phone rang, she snatched it
up nervously, then paused a moment before she uttered
a cautious, "Hello."

"Marjo?"

It was Matt. A sharp, yearning ache sliced through
her as her heart hammered in her chest and the breath
seemed pressed from her lungs.

"Marjo?"

She finally found breath to whisper, "Yes."

"What the hell is this damn note supposed to mean?"
he exploded.

She stood clutching the phone, silent, while her
throat tightened and her eyes burned with a sensation
that seemed so familiar it must be a natural state. But if
she let herself cry, she knew, she would never stop. If
the dam broke on her emotions, there would be no controlling the flood of feelings.

"Dammit, I've given you five days to figure things
out with Opie—and I've been going crazy waiting for
you to call. And then the day we're supposed to have a
lesson I get this snotty little note in the mail that sounds
like it was written by somebody's secretary!" He was so
angry his voice was shaking. There was a quaver of
emotion as he finished, "And dammit, what the hell do
you think you're saying?"

Oh, Matt. I need you. I miss you. The words in her
mind were so poignantly real that she was afraid she'd
say them aloud. She jerked the phone away from her

face and held it in both hands pressed between her breasts. The wall of the kitchen blurred in front of her, and her heart pounded so insistently that she pulled the receiver away from her chest, wondering if Matt had heard it.

"Marjo?" his voice repeated from the receiver, tiny and barely audible but still with the power to make her ache for him.

With a small sound that was not—could not be—a sob, she turned toward the phone and put the receiver back on the hook.

She stood staring at it until Opie's footsteps took her attention to the doorway.

"Who was that, Mom?" she asked, frowning at her mother.

"Just a—" She cleared her throat. "Just a wrong number, honey."

Opie regarded her pinched face and stiff shoulders for a long moment, then, still frowning, spun around and disappeared into the living room, leaving Marjo alone with her little white lie, her solitary emotions, and her unshed tears.

CHAPTER TEN

IN THE DAYS that followed, Marjo went through the motions of living, but she felt as lifeless and inanimate as the gravel that lined her training yard. She was more tired than she had been even at the times when Stan had abandoned them and she had worked twelve hours a day to pay the bills. But then she'd been fueled by anger. Now she felt only weary, drained by the effort to keep her emotions locked into a part of herself that she shared with no one.

And she felt as though she'd lost her daughter, as well as Matt. Opie was polite, helpful, and careful of her mother's feelings, but there was a distance between them that Marjo seemed unable to bridge. Opie avoided asking about either Matt or her father—as if the subjects were somehow forbidden in the household. Marjo could not get beyond her reserved, self-contained exterior, nor could she shake off the accusing, guilt-laden voice that nagged her with self-recrimination.

Grooming Dicey one rainy afternoon, she found herself talking to the little cocker as if the dog could understand or offer advice. She stopped herself, then shrugged and lifted one corner of her mouth in a grim smile. "Oh, I guess I've proved I can make it on my own, all right," she told Dicey with bleak humor. "All I need is a dog to talk to."

But the independence she had worked so long for now seemed meaningless and lonely, and she had to force herself to remember why she'd wanted it.

The one moment that gave her a glimmer of hope came during a task she shared with Opie, changing the cedar chips in the kennel beds. After they'd worked together for an hour, a little of the constraint between them gave way to the good-natured grousing that had been their habit. Hoping that it would open the communication between them, Marjo mentioned tentatively, "I haven't seen you wear your new jellies, Ope."

The girl continued sweeping chips into one of the kennels, not looking up.

Marjo smiled awkwardly. "I guess they're not much use around here."

Opie gave her a swift, guarded look, then turned back to her broom and plied it energetically for a few seconds. "I threw them away, Mom," she said, her eyes on the floor. "I didn't like them that much."

Marjo glanced up in surprise at the unexpected admission, as the beginnings of hopeful relief shot through her. Maybe the gift hadn't meant so much to Opie. Maybe Opie had already started to forget. Maybe, Marjo thought, as she bit her lip to keep down familiar emotions, ten-year-old Opie was more resilient than her mother, and it would not be an eternity until Opie seemed happy and outgoing again.

And maybe then Marjo could forgive herself.

She clung to that desperate belief as the last week of May dragged by, made difficult and desolate by the associations that were everywhere in her work and in her life: Matt, looking over her kennel runs and joking about the gender of the Beckman's shepherd; Matt, standing in the yard watching Timmy with a father's pride; Matt, leaning over her desk, flirting with her and hiding it behind an irrepressible grin.

Sitting at the counter in the office one evening she reached for the phone, impelled by a lonely cry in her mind. But before she touched the instrument, she jerked her hand away from it, ashamed of the impulse. How many times in the past had she given in to loneliness and despair and her own weakness? And what had it led to but more heartbreak?

On the first of June, a Wednesday, she spent the morning cleaning the kitchen she'd neglected for two weeks, then stood in Opie's doorway, examining the room with grim assessment. It was a hodge-podge of discarded clothes, used arts and crafts supplies, and unsorted homework papers.

She should have insisted Opie clean it. But how could she, when she'd been so lethargic herself that she'd hardly managed to make a meal every night? With a sigh, she bent over to pick up the nearest dirty sweat shirt.

Two hours later, she was on her knees in front of the closet, pairing up shoes from the pile that had been dumped in the corner, when her fingers, poking through old sneakers and discarded slippers, brushed against a smooth and fine-textured piece of cloth.

A gleam of something white and reflective caught the dim light in the closet as Marjo pushed aside the shoes. At the bottom of the pile was a lumpy package wrapped in white satin. Frowning, Marjo reached for it, and with a small jolt of shock, recognized the lace trim: Opie's christening gown, a family heirloom given to her by her grandmother.

The package rustled as Marjo picked it up, and her stomach tightened with apprehension. The gown was wrapped with loving care around white tissue paper. Marjo's hand fell still while her heart started a painful, heavy hammering in her chest. Slowly, with shaking fingers, she pushed aside the tissue paper.

Nestled inside, wrapped in the most beautiful and valuable possession that Opie owned, and tucked away in the bottom of her closet where she thought no one would find them, were the pink jellies.

Marjo sank back on her heels, staring numbly at the pink plastic shoes Opie had claimed not to care about. Her hands trembled as memory took her back to the afternoon Opie had told her she'd thrown them away.

Opie had lied, because she knew that was what her mother wanted to hear. And then she'd hidden away the shoes—just as she'd hidden her feelings, her secret loyalty to her father, her fragile, breakable dreams.

The shoes blurred in front of Marjo's eyes, and the first tear dropped to the tissue paper with an almost inaudible tap. Then, without warning, a sob welled up in her throat, broke out, agonized and unstoppable, and became a torrent of grief.

She buried her face in her hands and wept as she had wanted to weep since that miserable Sunday when Matt had left.

Her body jerked and her shoulders shook spasmodically as the anguish she had tried so desperately to control poured out in a wild, uncontrollable flood. Tears streamed from her eyes, seeped through her fingers, and dampened the tissue paper around the plastic shoes Opie had hidden away from her, and she cried for Opie, for her own vain struggle to deny the inevitable, for the desperate loneliness of the past week.

When her crying had worn itself down to shuddering breaths, Marjo pressed her wet hands to her eyes, then lurched to her feet to reach for the tissues on Opie's bureau. She blew her nose and wiped her eyes; then, swallowing the last, hiccoughing sob, picked up the jellies and brought them out to the kitchen table.

She stood gazing down at them for a long moment,

fingering the white satin caressingly, considering what she knew she had to do. Then she took another shaky breath and reached for the phone to call her ex-husband.

The last slice of pink still lingered in the western sky when Marjo drove through the tree-lined streets of West Allis, where lights were winking on in the windows of rambling, comfortable ranch houses, and a few tardy children on bicycles headed home from games of Red Light/Green Light and Hide and Seek.

From Matt's house, the illuminated kitchen window cast a square of light onto the shadowed lawn as Marjo turned into the driveway and parked behind the Ford station wagon. She shut off the car and stared at the house for an interminable length of time before she wiped her damp palms on her jeans, replaced them on the steering wheel, and stared at the house again.

Go on! a voice in her head urged impatiently. *It won't get any easier.*

But she stayed where she was, holding her breath against the nervous tremors in her stomach, until the porch light flicked on and a silhouette inside the hall approached the door, peered out, then stopped, motionless, waiting for her to come in.

She wiped her palms again, then, before she could change her mind, jerked open the door, climbed out, then shut it, turning her back on the house for a moment before she spun around and started briskly up the walk.

Her steps slowed as she reached the stairs, hesitating more as she climbed each riser, and when the back door squeaked open, she had come to a halt one step below the landing, her hands pushed nervously into the sanctuary of her pockets.

Matt stood framed in the open doorway holding the screen door open, utterly still, absolutely silent. She could hear the liquid whistle of a towhee in the weeping willow, and the faint stirring of the tree's pendant branches, but she herself forgot to speak as she gazed up at him, her eyes drinking in every detail of him. He wore tan chinos, a white Oxford shirt rolled up at the cuffs to reveal the muscular forearms that had held her close, and open to the hollow of his throat, which she'd kissed with such ardent pleasure. Her gaze rose to his lips, slightly parted but unsmiling, then to his eyes, which gazed back at her steadily and seriously.

"Hi," she croaked in a pinched voice.

"Hi." As if the word had broken some spell, he moved, to step outside the door and let it swing shut behind him, his eyes not moving from Marjo's face.

"I—ah—just took a chance on your being home. Are you—in the middle of something?"

He studied her face for a moment longer before he shook his head, and the corners of his mouth lifted momentarily. "No—I was just cleaning up the supper dishes."

Marjo's eyes dropped to the concrete steps, then she looked back up at his face. "I wanted to say in person that I'm sorry for hanging up on you." She swallowed a hard lump of nervousness in the back of her throat, but kept her eyes on Matt's.

"That's all right." He pushed his own hands into his pockets while his gaze drifted down over her Picasso printed sweatshirt, then back to her face. "How's Opie doing?"

"She's with her father," Marjo said. She looked down again. "You were right. Opie was the one who wrote to her father—who wanted to see him. I realized when I found how much she cared about the—the jellies—that I had to let her see him. I think"—she gave a small, uncertain shrug, still with downcast eyes—"maybe he's changed. But even if Opie gets hurt again, I owe her the right to take that chance. I can't ask her to choose between her father and me."

She sensed his nod, sensed him searching her face as

he waited for her to go on, looking for some clue as to where she was heading.

But her courage temporarily failed. The towhee called again from the willow tree, and Marjo said nothing.

Finally, Matt asked, "Did you come just to tell me about Opie and her father, Marjo?"

Her gaze rose to the open neck of his shirt. There was a pulse beating there, faintly. She could imagine the smell of citrus, though she wasn't close enough to know if he was wearing it.

He had told her she could be as aggressive as she wanted, she reminded herself in desperate reassurance. She swallowed again as she studied the pulse at his throat and said huskily, "No. I came to see if you wanted to go stargazing."

There was an awful moment of silence, then she lifted her eyes to his mouth.

He was smiling, a slow, gradual curving of his mouth that set her heart beating like a drum against her ribcage.

"In the leaky boat?" he asked her.

"Maybe—" She let her breath out in a rush, her feelings trembling on the edge of bursting from her body. "Maybe we don't need the boat."

He reached for her and pulled her up the last step and hard against his body, and that beautiful, smiling mouth came down onto hers in a kiss that was at once promise and fulfillment. She wrapped her hands around his back and pressed him closer, glorying in the rough embrace as he ground his mouth against hers, thrust with his tongue, spread his hands wide on her back to hold her forcefully against him.

When finally he broke off the kiss, it was to bury his face in her neck as his hands roved down the length of her spine, then wrapped around her and squeezed. "I want more than just a night of stargazing, Marjo," he said hoarsely.

"Oh, God, so do I."

His hands came up to circle her face and tip it up to his as he raised his head to gaze down at her. "How much do you want, then?" he asked intently.

"As much as I can have." Her eyes were wide with vulnerable honesty. She covered his hands with her own, pressing her palms against the back of his knuckles. "I want—forever."

He brushed his hands back through her hair, and hers slid down to his wrists. His somber expression changed to a grin of wide, irrepressible satisfaction, and he promised, "You got it, Ms. Opaski."

Her tremulous smile widened with joyous abandon just before he kissed her again, at the same time reaching behind him for the screen door.

"I'm thinking," he murmured without lifting his mouth from hers, "that we don't need the boat, Ms. Opaski."

She smiled against his mouth as he walked backward with her toward the door. "Maybe," she murmured back, "we don't need the stars, either."

COMING NEXT MONTH

A LADY'S DESIRE #442
by Cait Logan

Dan Jones always puts business
before pleasure—until he meets Rainey
Dawn McDowell at a flea market. She has
what he wants so he follows her home...
to make an irresistable offer...

ROMANCING CHARLEY #443
by Hilary Cole

Free-lance reporter Charley
Channing literally runs into James
MacNamara, a newspaper columnist after
the same story. Mutually smitten, they
team up, but find they have very different
approaches to partnership...

SECOND CHANCE AT LOVE

Be Sure to Read These New Releases!

CODY'S GYPSY #438
by Courtney Ryan

Detective Cody Davis's newest assignment
is to locate the elusive Liza Carlisle, a free
spirit with a worried father. Cody finds her—
and falls for her. But will the beautiful
gypsy slow down so Cody can catch her...

THE LADY EVE #439
by Dana Daniels

Millionaire Tyler Lightfoot is intrigued
by Shelly Hayes, adorable and
irrepressible. But, it seems, all the men in
town are interested! As jealousy and
desire abound, a sudden obstacle throws Ty
and Shelly into a legal stalemate,
and a sensual onslaught...

Order on opposite page!

SECOND CHANCE AT LOVE

___ 0-425-10080-4	CONSPIRACY OF HEARTS #406 Pat Dalton	$2.25
___ 0-425-10081-2	HEAT WAVE #407 Lee Williams	$2.25
___ 0-425-10082-0	TEMPORARY ANGEL #408 Courtney Ryan	$2.25
___ 0-425-10083-9	HERO AT LARGE #409 Steffie Hall	$2.25
___ 0-425-10084-7	CHASING RAINBOWS #410 Carole Buck	$2.25
___ 0-425-10085-5	PRIMITIVE GLORY #411 Cass McAndrew	$2.25
___ 0-425-10225-4	TWO'S COMPANY #412 Sherryl Woods	$2.25
___ 0-425-10226-2	WINTER FLAME #413 Kelly Adams	$2.25
___ 0-425-10227-0	A SWEET TALKIN' MAN #414 Jackie Leigh	$2.25
___ 0-425-10228-9	TOUCH OF MIDNIGHT #415 Kerry Price	$2.25
___ 0-425-10229-7	HART'S DESIRE #416 Linda Raye	$2.25
___ 0-425-10230-0	A FAMILY AFFAIR #417 Cindy Victor	$2.25
___ 0-425-10513-X	CUPID'S CAMPAIGN #418 Kate Gilbert	$2.50
___ 0-425-10514-8	GAMBLER'S LADY #419 Cait Logan	$2.50
___ 0-425-10515-6	ACCENT ON DESIRE #420 Christa Merlin	$2.50
___ 0-425-10516-4	YOUNG AT HEART #421 Jackie Leigh	$2.50
___ 0-425-10517-2	STRANGER FROM THE PAST #422 Jan Mathews	$2.50
___ 0-425-10518-0	HEAVEN SENT #423 Jamisan Whitney	$2.50
___ 0-425-10530-X	ALL THAT JAZZ #424 Carole Buck	$2.50
___ 0-425-10531-8	IT STARTED WITH A KISS #425 Kit Windham	$2.50
___ 0-425-10558-X	ONE FROM THE HEART #426 Cinda Richards	$2.50
___ 0-425-10559-8	NIGHTS IN SHINING SPLENDOR #427 Christina Dair	$2.50
___ 0-425-10560-1	ANGEL ON MY SHOULDER #428 Jackie Leigh	$2.50
___ 0-425-10561-X	RULES OF THE HEART #429 Samantha Quinn	$2.50
___ 0-425-10604-7	PRINCE CHARMING REPLIES #430 Sherryl Woods	$2.50
___ 0-425-10605-5	DESIRE'S DESTINY #431 Jamisan Whitney	$2.50
___ 0-425-10680-2	A LADY'S CHOICE #432 Cait Logan	$2.50
___ 0-425-10681-0	CLOSE SCRUTINY #433 Pat Dalton	$2.50
___ 0-425-10682-9	SURRENDER THE DAWN #434 Jan Mathews	$2.50
___ 0-425-10683-7	A WARM DECEMBER #435 Jacqueline Topaz	$2.50
___ 0-425-10708-6	RAINBOW'S END #436 Carole Buck	$2.50
___ 0-425-10709-4	TEMPTRESS #437 Linda Raye	$2.50
___ 0-425-10743-4	CODY'S GYPSY #438 Courtney Ryan	$2.50
___ 0-425-10744-2	THE LADY EVE #439 Dana Daniels	$2.50
___ 0-425-10836-8	RELEASED INTO DAWN #440 Kelly Adams	$2.50
___ 0-425-10837-6	STAR LIGHT, STAR BRIGHT #441 Frances West	$2.50
___ 0-425-10873-2	A LADY'S DESIRE #442 Cait Logan (On sale July '88)	$2.50
___ 0-425-10874-0	ROMANCING CHARLEY #443 Hilary Cole (On sale July '88)	$2.50

Please send the titles I've checked above. Mail orders to:

BERKLEY PUBLISHING GROUP
390 Murray Hill Pkwy., Dept. B
East Rutherford, NJ 07073

NAME_____

ADDRESS_____

CITY_____

STATE_____ZIP_____

Please allow 6 weeks for delivery.
Prices are subject to change without notice.

POSTAGE & HANDLING:
$1.00 for one book, $.25 for each
additional. Do not exceed $3.50.

BOOK TOTAL $_____

SHIPPING & HANDLING $_____

APPLICABLE SALES TAX $_____
(CA, NJ, NY, PA)

TOTAL AMOUNT DUE $_____
PAYABLE IN US FUNDS.
(No cash orders accepted.)